NOW THROUGH LABOR DAY

Kayli Schaaf

—For Sweet Martha, always

TABLE OF CONTENTS

DAY ONE

In retrospect, the State Fair wasn't the best place for a third date. I liked Eric, but as he walked past fried pickles and Pronto Pups in search of lean protein, I knew things weren't going to work out between us.

Eric was new to Minnesota, and I was new to Bumble. When we were matched, all five of his photos were of him outdoors—hiking, camping, fishing—and while those things weren't high on my personal priorities, I was intrigued by how happy he looked doing them.

Our first date was a walk around Bde Maka Ska. He lived in Elon in Uptown like every other newly minted professional working downtown. We stopped for a beer at Lyn Lake Brewery. My hopes hadn't been high, but I left the bar with a smile on my face, and when he texted two days later, I said yes to a second date.

We spent half a Sunday hiking the bluffs in Frontenac State Park. I didn't have the right shoes and could hardly walk the next day, but the exertion made me deliriously happy. When we reached the cliff's edge, I was breathless and sweaty and in awe of the beauty in front of me. He kissed me and asked me out again, and I immediately agreed.

The State Fair had been my choice. It was my favorite time of year, watching summer turn into fall, and nothing made me happier than a bucket of cookies and a mini-donut beer alongside a hundred thousand of Minnesota's best.

But Eric didn't get it. He was a New Yorker, born and raised. If he wanted street food and to people watch, all he had to do was walk out his front door. To him, it looked like I waited all year for something that mildly annoyed him at home.

It was night one of the twelve day run of the fair. I didn't know if I'd get back again, so I wanted to hit my mainstays, like the flowering onion and Minneapple pie, but Eric was placating me at best.

I didn't know what to do about it. He checked his smartwatch constantly and it had crossed from distracting to irritating after about an hour. I looked at him in his polo and chinos, his white sneakers covered in dirt and food and probably horseshit, and I sighed. He was cute and smart and motivated, but he wasn't for me.

Out of a sense of responsibility, I helped him find something to eat at a chicken grill underneath the Grandstand walkway I'd never seen before. He got a chicken and rice bowl and walked with me while I tried to get back into my routine, but the magic of the fair was gone. After my second mini-donut beer, I got the courage to do what I should have done hours before.

"Eric," I said. "You hate this."

He froze, then shrugged and nodded. "Yeah," he admitted, pushing his sunglasses up onto his head. "I guess it's not my thing."

"Go home," I told him. "Or go out. Go do what you want."

"Annie," he started, but I waved him off.

"I want to be here. You don't. I'm good with that," I shrugged.

"I just—" he said, cutting himself off. "Annie, no one here is that honest." I shrugged. "But if you're sure…"

"I'm sure," I nodded, shifting my weight to the balls of my feet.

"Okay," he said. "I'll call you." He leaned forward and kissed my cheek, sloshing my beer onto my shoes.

"No, you won't," I said under my breath, shrugging again, but found myself mostly unbothered. I felt a sense of freedom watching him go, knowing I could do exactly what I wanted. At that moment, I wanted a fudge puppy and to find a good bench to watch the sunset. The lights would be coming on shortly so I wanted to walk the Midway and watch the crowd change from families to teenagers and young adults, and I'd probably get one more beer before walking home.

I made my way slowly towards Coasters, my hopes unreasonably high that I might find an empty tilt-a-whirl table to sit at while the sun came down. I was halfway there when I heard my name, and it stopped me in my tracks.

It had been ten years since I'd heard his voice; maybe five since I'd last Googled him, but before I turned I knew who it would be. "Holy shit," he said. "Annie Banannie."

"Brody?" I said, pushing my sunglasses into my hair. He was tall—so tall—somewhere on the high end of six feet, and his shoulders were so wide that they stretched the bright yellow shirt he wore. He was self-consciously removing a hairnet, stuffing it into the pocket of the black jeans he wore, and I caught a couple of tattoos on his forearm, nearly impossible to make out against his brown skin in the low light.

I was tongue-tied, and I knew it. The last time I'd seen Brody Washington, days before Christmas nearly ten years prior, his sister had died. Two weeks before that, he'd been my first kiss.

"Hi," I finally said, taking a step towards him. We were blocking the other pedestrians, getting more than one annoyed sigh as they side-stepped us, so I

7

gripped his tattooed forearm and pulled him aside, directly next to the Big Fat Bacon stand.

We both started to speak at the same time, then faltered. I ignored the thump that my heart made when he smiled, and he gestured for me to go first. "What are you doing here?" I asked him. The question was a stupid one. He clearly worked within the fairgrounds, but I didn't know what else to say, what else there was that didn't hurt.

"Making some extra money," he said. "I've done this the last couple of years. Get a couple grease burns, make some extra cash. Works out okay. What about you? Are you alone? Did I drag you away from friends?"

I shook my head. "No," I faltered again. Was it more depressing that I was alone or that I'd sent my date off for being less than thrilled about the fair overall? I shook my head. I didn't see any reason to lie, even if I felt some need to save face in front of Brody and those big brown eyes of his.

"I was on a date," I admitted. "Sent him on his way when he wasn't into being here."

Brody's laugh was as melodic as I remembered. My heart thumped so hard again I wondered if I might have been experiencing indigestion. "Haven't changed a bit," he shook his head.

I rolled my eyes playfully. "In some ways, no, I suppose not."

He caught my gaze and nodded. "Where are you headed right now?"

"Coasters," I said. "Midway'll be lighting up. I want to watch it."

"I've got about fifteen minutes to kill. Do you mind if I join you?"

"Please," I encouraged him. There was an awkward silence, one where I knew we were both hesitating to ask the questions that were on our minds, but he let me speak first.

"How's your family?" I asked softly.

He squeezed my shoulder briefly. He smelled like grease and onions. "We're doing okay," he said. "My mom and step-dad—they're still married. You know what kinda feat that is, after everything."

I nodded. "And you?" I asked.

"I'm good, Annie," he said. "Got a day job. Get to see my family whenever I want to. I talk to Gwen when I can. Ten years," he shook his head. "If I could go back and tell fourteen-year-old me that I'd survive losing her, I would. I think I would have done a lot differently."

I bit down on the inside of my lip, but we arrived at Coasters just as a small family left one of the tilt-a-whirl tables. Without a word, Brody knew I wanted one of those tables, so I followed him to it, slipping in on the other side.

In front of me, the sky was a canvas of pinks and oranges. It was a sunset I would have loved to photograph, but in that moment, my attention was elsewhere.

"And you," my gaze turned abruptly to the sunset in front of us. "You're healthy." He said it like a statement rather than a question.

"As a horse," I said after a long moment, pulling my long, dark ponytail over my shoulder without thought.

"Surgery worked," he said and again it wasn't a question.

I nodded. "Twice," I replied after a moment.

He sucked in a breath. "It came back?"

I nodded again. "When I was sixteen."

He looked a million miles away and I knew he probably was. Gwen had been my roommate at Children's Hospital when we were both preteens. I hadn't been easy to get along with, hormonal and angry that I was twelve with bone cancer, but she'd ignored my attempts to shut her down, and eventually I stop resisting her. And Brody—I stopped resisting him too.

I was diagnosed at eleven with osteosarcoma, a very rare type of bone cancer that appeared in my left arm. It took a combination of chemo and surgery to get rid of it and a whole lot of rehab to relearn how to use my arm, but I survived it once at twelve and again at sixteen, when it appeared again in my other arm. Gwen had a tumor pushing on her frontal lobe and she hadn't survived the surgery to remove it.

I thought about her a lot, even ten years later. Brody still popped into my thoughts too, whenever I read an article about first kisses and first crushes. I hadn't been well enough to attend her funeral, my own surgery only a few days out, and when the Washingtons left the hospital, I never saw any of them again.

"How's your mom?" he asked after another silence.

"She's doing well," I said. "Working hard."

"Still living in Willmar?" I nodded. "What about you?" he asked.

"I'm close enough to walk home," I said, looking north for a moment.

"Nice," he said, drifting away again. "You know," he continued, his cadence quicker. "I probably have thought about you every couple of weeks for ten years."

I smiled, watching as the first set of Midway rides lit up, reds and greens and blues against the deepening pink of the sky behind them. "You were my first kiss, Brody," I shook my head teasingly. "You were basically all I thought of during physical therapy."

He snorted, shifting beside me. I looked over at him and he opened his mouth to speak again, but we were interrupted by two people in the same yellow shirt and dark jeans that Brody had on.

"Dude," the guy said. He looked a couple years younger than Brody, maybe closer to my age. "We gotta go. Now. Monica just texted 911."

"Pretty sure that's a grease fire, or theft, or one of her ex-husbands showed up," the girl, a cute blonde added. She took one look at me and turned back to Brody.

Brody looked from me to them and the girl rolled her eyes. I decided to save him the trouble of an awkward exit and spoke. "Real friends don't disregard 911 texts," I said. "It was great to see you, Brody. Go."

"Brody?" the girl asked.

"Come on, man. She gets it," the guy said.

Brody was flustered and I couldn't blame him. His friends were demanding and we'd finally found our groove conversationally, but the moment was gone. He rose from his side of the tilt-a-whirl table, nearly knocking his head on the top of it. "Thanks for the fifteen minutes," he said.

"Anytime," I assured him. His friends nearly dragged him away, but I turned back to the Midway, not wanting to watch him go. I thought about Gwen frequently, but I'd let the grief go. Having Brody in front of me brought a lot of that to the surface.

"...right back," I heard his voice again. "I just need a second."

He was abruptly in front of me, his smile small and hesitant, and when he kissed me , I wasn't surprised. His lips were soft, his face rough with a closely trimmed beard I hadn't been able to see against his skin. His hand was on my cheek when we parted. "Wanted to be your first and last, if only for a little while." His grin was as wolfish as I remembered and when he walked towards his friends, they were staring at him in disbelief.

I watched him go this time. I lost him after about five seconds as he melted into the crowd, and I was unable to stop the grin from spreading across my face.

DAY TWO

I hadn't realized I was looking for him until Yvette called me out on it. We'd both worked late mid shifts, wrapping up our manager shifts at Target around eight. We'd been flirting with attending the fair all day, making jokes about how we wished we were the illegally parked people taking up all of the empty space in our parking lot and eating fried foods instead of selling groceries.

Yvette Vang was a Minnesota girl too, but new to the Saint Paul suburbs, having grown up on the Iron Range and completed college in Duluth. She and I had attended Target's business college together, going through our training at a neighboring store in the east metro before we'd both been given permanent jobs at the Roseville store.

We got along well from the beginning, which was a feat for me, even as an adult. When I was sick, my mom said I wore my illness like armor. I refused to allow people in. It was easy for me to understand that it was a form of self-protection, especially when there was so much to lose, but I still struggled with it as an adult.

I never was good at small talk. I didn't know how to engage people when I wasn't truly sure I was interested in talking to them at all. It made my adult friendships as rare as my childhood ones. But Yvette was easy to like because she was nothing like me. Small talk was her forte. People loved talking to her. She was the slowest cashier in our store because she'd happily hear the guest's life story if they were inclined to share it. If they weren't, she'd share hers. She didn't have an off-switch that made her stop talking or identify awkward situations, so she powered through them without knowing.

The first time we spoke, she reminded me so much of Gwen that I stopped by Gwen's gravesite for the first time in years. I thought I was happiest alone until I met Gwen—she and Brody showed me how untrue that was. Yvette was quickly on her way to the same status.

She lived in an apartment in Inver Grove Heights and rather than drive home to change, she bought a whole new outfit and followed me to my Falcon Heights studio, slipping out of her red and khaki for a summer dress and a denim vest.

I took more care with my outfit than I normally did. It was another indicator that I was out for more than another trip to the fair, but I didn't catch it until Yvette called me out in front of the dairy barn.

"Okay, who are you looking for?" she asked me, sipping from her strawberry shake. The sun was down, the fair neon and rowdy, and I took a step back, not from her accusation but the realization that it was true.

"I'm... not," I said lamely, shrugging helplessly.

"Sweetheart, we've put in—" she glanced at the fitness tracker on her wrist, "—almost eight thousand steps and we've been here an hour. You haven't eaten anything. Who are you trying to find?"

"I don't know," I said. "I don't know that that's what I'm even trying to do."

"Bullshit," she said cheerfully. "You're totally looking for someone. Who?"

"I ran into someone last night." The words spilled out It felt like my mouth had betrayed my brain.

"Before or after you kicked your date to the curb?" she said, grinning widely.

I rolled my eyes. Yvette was the reason I'd joined Bumble in the first place so she hadn't believed I was serious when I told her I'd sent Eric on his way so I

14

could enjoy my night in peace. It took a while to convince her I was telling the truth, and then she had laughed so long we'd gotten some looks from other team members at work.

"After," I said. "Someone I used to know, I guess."

"What makes you think he'll be here?"

"How do you know it's a guy?"

It was her turn to roll her eyes. "Because I'm not stupid," she teased. "Who is he?"

"Someone I used to know," I shrugged. "He said he works here for extra cash. I didn't realize I was looking for him until you pointed it out."

"Used to know in what way?" Yvette said. "Biblically, or…"

"Evie, I was twelve when I saw him last," I deadpanned and she burst into giggles. "So no, not biblically. We were friends. That's all."

"Not all," she shook her head.

"What?"

"You're lying," she said, shrugging. "You have a tell, you know."

"Oh come on," I shook my head, but I was running through the motions I'd made, eye contact I'd broken, and I couldn't come up with anything.

"I'm not telling you what it is," she said. "But you have one. And you're lying."

I was lying. About a lot more than Brody being the first guy I kissed. No one in my adult life had any idea I was a sick child, Yvette included. There was never a place in the bio that made any sense to add it in, so I never did. The couple of friends I'd made in college never knew I'd spent my teenage years fighting cancer; certainly no one at Target knew it. It wasn't easy to explain how important Brody was in my life without knowing about the experience of losing Gwen, of how sick I had been, but I didn't want to share it, not even with Yvette.

I could give her something, though. Maybe she'd know I was still hiding something, maybe not, but it would give her something to hold on to while she considered how much effort it was to be my friend.

I hadn't been able to stop thinking about it anyway, about how all the ways he'd kissed me the first time were so similar to the way he had the previous night. He'd been avoiding me at the time a decade earlier and I hadn't been sure why, but I wasn't going to be the one to tell him it hurt, so I let him drift away like it wasn't painful for me.

My mom had brought me a new scarf, a cashmere blend, name-brand scarf meant to placate me for not being around as much as she wished she could be, and I accepted the gift and the apology without thought. I had just wrapped it around my neck when Gwen and Brody arrived.

I wouldn't make eye contact with him, but I had been aware of his eyes on me. Ultimately, it'd been Gwen who broke the tension, invading my personal space to touch the scarf. She told Brody how soft it was, encouraged him to touch it, and she was pushing my mom out the door before I could process what was happening.

I had been watching them leave, so I hadn't expected Brody to take Gwen's spot in my personal space until he was in it. He reached for the scarf, his fingers catching my jaw, and froze in anticipation.

I recognized the moment for what it was about to be. In my head, I had cataloged everything. His fingers slipped to my cheek and he cupped it with his hand, his touch so gentle it felt like a dream. He was holding his breath and it bolstered my courage—I reached forward and pressed my hand against his heart.

I was the one to close the space between us, to press my lips hesitantly against his. I remembered that his eyes widened, then closed, and it was clumsy and sweet and embarrassing and everything a first kiss should be. Our last kiss was different, both of us with a decade of practice under our belts, but the gentle way he'd touched me gave me a significant sense of déjà vu. It was why I hadn't been able to stop thinking about it, or him, and it took me a long moment to clear it out of my head enough to offer Yvette any information.

"He was my first kiss," I finally said. She practically swooned at me, her dark eyes wide and bright. "And, uh… also my last."

She looked at me strangely. "I really hope you're not telling me the last guy you kissed was ten years ago."

I rolled my eyes. "Not telling you that," I said. "I've already told you things that would contradict that anyway."

She held up her hands, the strawberry shake dripping down her fingers. "Then what?"

"He kissed me again. Last night."

"He did no such thing!" she shrieked. "What? You didn't get his number? You haven't found him online? What the hell is wrong with you?"

"I tried," I admitted. And I had. He had no social media presence whatsoever besides an ancient MySpace account. If there were others, they were locked up tight, though I thought it was more likely that he didn't have them. The Brody I'd known before Gwen died enjoyed casually disregarding societal expectations—back then, he would let Gwen and I paint his fingernails, and he made no apologies for it. I could see how forgoing social media would give him the same kind of thrill.

17

"So what's the plan?" Yvette asked after I gave her the details of the previous night. "No Insta page, so we've gotta go off the grid."

I shook my head, unable to keep the laughter in. "What are you even saying? Off what grid?"

"We know some things, Annie," she said excitedly. "We're looking for a wide receiver in a yellow shirt."

I laughed. "We're not looking for anyone. It's stupid. I didn't even realize I was doing it until you pointed it out."

"But you were," she pointed out. "It'll be fun. Like a State Fair scavenger hunt."

I shook my head. "He may not be on social media, but I am. If he wants to find me, it wouldn't be hard." She opened her mouth to argue, but I continued before she could say anything else. I felt like I wouldn't be hard to convince, and that felt mostly pathetic to me. "You're right; I haven't eaten anything. Let's go find me a beer."

"…that's not food," Yvette teased.

"Better than food," I joked and she laughed.

"I'm keeping my eyes peeled," she told me. "Don't argue with me. I'm looking for him."

"Knock yourself out," I told her, my stomach fluttering nervously.

Being called out for looking for Brody was unnerving; it hadn't been an intentional move on my part. Brody hadn't been on my mind during the day; work had kept me focused, and after losing him at the fair the night before, I didn't dwell. I took the couple of photos I'd been itching to capture, I had a sangria beer and a mac and cheese cupcake, and I walked the half mile home.

So maybe it hadn't been intentional, but he was definitely buried in my subconscious. I'd picked my favorite jeans and a deep green top I only ever wore when I was trying to impress someone. I shook my head. It didn't matter. At least one hundred thousand people passed through the fairground gates every day. Seeing him again would be unlikely at best.

Yvette and I wandered slowly towards Ballpark Café and I mulled over my beer options. I left her alone for no longer than five minutes, but when I found her, she was chatting with a middle-aged fair employee in a blue tee shirt like she was a long lost friend.

"Annie," Yvette said, her smile wide and mischievous. "This is Sue. She's worked for the fair for twenty-five years. Can you imagine?"

"Sounds like my dream job," I admitted and Sue laughed. I wasn't kidding, but I smiled at her anyway.

"I was asking Sue if she knew which vendors wear yellow," Yvette continued.

I knew that from the moment I saw them together and I sighed. Sue didn't know what to think about me. Yvette's warmth made me look colder by comparison.

"There are a lot of vendors that wear yellow," Sue said when I didn't speak and I nodded. The look Yvette gave me was the closest to a glare I'd ever seen her make.

"Sweet Martha's and the fry stands are the most obvious," I said. "But they were wearing plain yellow shirts, and I know those two stands are branded."

Yvette raised her eyebrows in surprise and I sighed again. It was something else I hadn't realized I'd catalogued until I said it out loud. "It doesn't matter," I said. "Thank you for your help."

Sue's gaze was hard to meet. "Who's this guy to you?"

"Someone I knew a lifetime ago," I told her, desperate for the conversation to end.

"Honey, you haven't lived long enough for lifetimes," she said softly. It was meant to be encouraging, but it wasn't. I'd been through more than most at twenty-two.

"You'd be wrong about that," was all I could say. "Thank you again."

I walked away from both Sue and Yvette, knowing the latter would follow me. "Let it go," I said when I felt her at my elbow.

"I don't understand you," she said, the closest to irritable I'd ever heard her.

"I know," I said. "I don't know that I'm meant to be understood."

"You're allowed to be happy," she said. "Sometimes I feel like you don't think you are."

"Brody isn't what makes me happy, Evie," I pointed out. "And he's not why I'm here. Come on. Let's go on the Skyride."

She gave me a look that told me she knew exactly what I was doing. "You're bribing me," she said.

"It's your favorite way to see the fair. So let's go," I said again.

She held my gaze for a moment before she nodded. "Fine," she said. "But we didn't have to run away from Sue like that. Imagine the stories she's got after twenty-five years. That would be something to hear."

It was how Yvette thought of all of her interactions with other people. She wanted to know their stories, to understand what drove them. Not for the first time, I thought she was in the wrong career. She was meant to listen and to motivate in a way she wasn't being challenged to do.

"Next time," I promised. "I'll ask."

"Bullshit," she laughed. "My antisocial bestie asking anything of anyone she doesn't already know? I don't think so."

I jolted in response. She'd easily become the best friend I'd had in years, but I had not considered I represented the same thing to her.

She wrapped an arm around my shoulders, her smile soft, but she was smart enough not to say anything about it. If I wasn't good with people, I was worse with emotional moments. Yvette didn't have to know much about me to understand that.

"So Skyride?" she said.

"Definitely," I replied and I let her lead the way.

DAY THREE

I woke on Saturday morning to a sharp knock on my apartment door. It was early, before eight, and Yvette and I had closed down the fair, so I was in no shape for early-morning visitors. I stuffed my face into my pillow to block out the sun streaming in from the window above my bed, but the knock came again, and I sighed in frustration and took the four steps across my apartment to pull open the door.

"Mom?" I said in surprise. The door caught on the chain lock, so I shut it again, unlatched the security lock, and opened the door wide.

She stepped in hesitantly, seemingly aware for the first time that she could have been interrupting something. I was in a sports bra and shorts, and I realized quickly that Yvette and I had just tossed our clothes on the floor before we'd gone to bed. I opened my mouth to speak just as Yvette popped up from my bed, looking around in confusion.

"Shit," she rubbed her eyes. "What time is it?"

For maybe the first time in my mother's life, she was speechless. Yvette was wearing one of my shirts, an oversized Gophers shirt I'd gotten at a football game and was in my bed. I knew what it looked like, and I couldn't help it—I started to laugh.

"Oh no," Yvette said, connecting the dots. "Mama Jenkins, your daughter is only into dudes."

I snorted, leaning against the bed as I laughed harder. My mom didn't really believe otherwise, having known me better than most mothers knew their daughters at twenty-two, but I knew she wouldn't put it past me to experiment, and she had no idea what she could have walked in on.

Yvette squinted at my microwave and cringed. "Shit," she said again. "I have to be at work in two hours." She rolled out of bed, the shirt long, but not long enough for to stop my mother from understanding she was only wearing underwear beneath it.

"Oh lord," I said, putting my face in my hands. "Evie, there are shorts in the dresser. Second drawer."

She laughed and my mom rolled her eyes, but I could see how happy she was that I'd finally found someone else to open up to. Yvette grabbed a pair of denim shorts at random and slid into them, loose and long on her but they would do the job. She grabbed her dress and vest from the floor, kissed my forehead, and she was gone.

"I suppose I should start calling first," my mom said after an extended silence.

I started to laugh again and I found it hard to control it. I dug my own shirt out of my dresser and slid into it, leaning against my bed. "You got a day off," I said.

She nodded. "And I wanted to see you. You need to call me more."

"I call you every other day," I pointed out teasingly. "I think I need to call you less."

"You didn't tell me how your date went," she said. "I know what third dates mean, Annabel."

I snorted so loudly it turned into a cough. It took me a moment to collect myself. "Maybe on TV, Mom. Good god."

"Go take a shower," she said. "We're going out and you're going to tell me about it."

"Mom," I complained. "There's nothing to tell."

"Shower," she pointed and I playfully knocked her hand down, but I complied.

My mom and I lived about three hours apart, but we talked nearly daily, both working odd hours because of customer-service jobs—she was a store manager of the Cub Foods in Willmar. We didn't see

23

each other as frequently as either of us would have liked. It had been her suggestion to look at Target for a job, her insistence that I attend college in the Cities, and as afraid as I was to do it all on my own, I obliged her.

I'd put her through hell when I was sick. I was bad at twelve, angry and upset and mean, but it was nothing compared to the nightmare I'd become at sixteen. I had next to no one, spending over a year after my first surgery in physical therapy to rehab my arm. Going to high school alone—friendless and sickly—I was horrible to her. But when my cancer returned in my right arm, I became something cruel. The surgery was harder on me the second time, the recovery time worse, and I never went back to school, getting my diploma just before my seventeenth birthday through a tutor.

I didn't know how to manage my anger or my fear. I had nearly died during the second surgery, my immune system compromised after multiple chemo treatments, and I had been sick for a long time, but I had never felt like death was something I would have to face. It took a long time for me to come out of that—it took college, time and separation and the abrupt understanding that because no one knew I had been sick, no one would make excuses for my behavior.

I struggled through college mostly alone. I wasn't used to a classroom setting after so much upheaval as a teen, and I had to work hard to get the grades I wanted; I wasn't aware that I was missing much until my senior year. It was the first time I'd had a roommate I liked. Paula was laid back, which was what I needed to come out of my shell. She didn't ask much of me, didn't treat me like I was strange for being a loner, so she made me less of one.

I went home less that year than any other. I had my first real boyfriend, and then decided I didn't want the emotions that came with a boyfriend, and found other uses for the guys on campus. It was the most normal I'd ever felt.

It was coming home less that made my relationship with my mom flourish. She felt less responsible for my happiness, and I found it easier to share the details of my life when I wasn't looking at her. It took a long time for me to get up the courage to apologize to her for the despicable things I'd said to her and blamed her for. As easily as she let it go, it made me think she hadn't internalized all of the things I'd said, but when I saw her, I knew she had. There was something in her expression that I struggled to identify, but eventually I could see how wary she was. She didn't know if I would backslide to the person I'd been before.

I came out of the bathroom in a towel. My mom was brewing coffee in my Keurig. "Where are we going?" I asked her.

"It's been probably twenty years since I've gone to the fair. I bought tickets," she said and I let out a sound that was something between a laugh and a groan.

"What?" she asked.

"Nothing," I shook my head. "Fair. Okay." I reached into my closet for an old tee shirt and denim shorts, completely aware that I was underdressing after overdressing the night before.

I skipped makeup and pulled my hair into a messy bun. My mom raised her eyebrows, but I shrugged as I slipped into a pair of canvas flats. I'd tell her about Brody eventually—that was unavoidable—but she and Brody's mom, Alissa, had gotten close before Gwen died. I knew it hurt her when the Washington family disappeared from our lives. Gwen was gone and they didn't want to look at me—it wasn't like either of us could hold that against them, but it didn't make it hurt less.

"Tell me about your friend," my mom said.

"Yvette?" I asked. "We work together."

"You like her."

"Yes, Mom. She's my friend. I like her," I paused, but again, meeting my mom's gaze, I knew what she was thinking. "I really don't spend all of my time alone. I'm okay."

She tilted her head to look at me, her dark eyes taking me in. She and I didn't look much alike—my dark hair and green eyes came from a father I didn't remember, one who'd died when I was a toddler. It was the shape of our mouths that we had in common and with that came the same nervous gestures. She was biting on the inside of her lip, but she blew out a breath before I could dissect it.

"You do seem okay," she finally said.

"Is that why you're here?" I asked. "To check on me?"

"My entire reason for existing is to check on you, Annie," she teased. "But you've been harder to reach, and I was worried. Seems like it might actually be a good thing."

"Mom," I said, shaking my head. "We talked two days ago."

"For half a minute," she pointed out. "Don't fault me for worrying about you."

"You've spent enough time worrying about me," I said. "I'm fine."

She closed her eyes for a moment and I knew the conversation could go one of two ways. She could dwell, bring up how scared she had been when I was sick, how terrified she'd been when I was recovering, and we could go down the path that led to the darkest parts of both of our lives. It was that, or it was moving on. It was trusting me. The latter would be harder for her, even given how much our relationship had improved.

"I didn't tell you about my date," I said, helping her along to the second option, "Because it wasn't worth talking about."

"Why not?" She asked. "What'd you do?"

"I took him to the fair," I said and she laughed.

"That's what that groan was for earlier then?"

"Not quite," I said, my thoughts drifting to Brody again. "I'll get there. But let's go." I poured her coffee into a disposable cup and I led the way, walking towards Snelling. It was eight o'clock and already hot. It would probably make for a short trip, which was probably best given how much Brody was already on my mind.

I told my mom about sending Eric on his way, about enjoying the fair, and I sighed before I got to what needed to be said. "I ran into Brody Washington."

My mom stopped for a moment, looking at me in surprise. "Goodness," she put a hand to her chest. Thinking about Gwen was hard for her. It made her think of how easily she could have lost me, on top of the sadness of losing Alissa's friendship. "How's he?"

"He said good," I told her. "He's got a side job somewhere here," I gestured in front of us where the fair loomed. "I don't know where. We talked for a few minutes and he went back to work."

She looked at me for a moment, a small smile on her lips. "How handsome did that boy end up?"

I shook my head and groaned again. "Unbelievably. Ugh. Mom, he kissed me."

She started to laugh and I poked her in the side. "That's not funny. That was mean. I keep thinking about him. I don't want to think about him. It makes me uncomfortable."

"Because you're not in control of it," she said, grabbing the finger I was poking her with. "And you hate not being in control." I couldn't argue with that. After everything, I preferred to manage my own affairs with few surprises. Brody had been a big one. "And that boy has always thrown off your equilibrium."

"He should have to be ugly," I grumbled. "He was gorgeous at fourteen. Ugh."

She laughed again and clapped her hands happily. "Oh Annie," she said. "Don't hold it against me, but I love this."

"Holding. A little," I told her.

"You've always been too grown up. You sound your age. Don't hold it against me to be happy about that," she said.

"Being my age sucks."

She laughed again and I couldn't stop my smile. "We can look for him."

I shook my head. "You sound like Evie. No."

She raised her eyebrows at me, so I explained that we'd attended the fair the night before and she snickered gleefully. "What does he look like?" she asked, not quite achieving the innocent tone she was going for.

"Shut up, Mom," I rolled my eyes. "We're not looking for him."

"Fine," she held up her hands in surrender. "But I still want to know."

"Like Brody ten years older," I crossed my arms over my chest, letting her hand our tickets over to the attendant at the gate. She gave me another look. "Fine. He looks like Brody ten years older if Brody had been spending the last ten years working on becoming a damn tight end. He's tall and fit and he still has that stupid smile and those eyes, and a goddamn beard that I could basically just…" I trailed off, recalling abruptly that I was talking to my mother. She snorted. "He's stunning. Because he wasn't ever going to be anything but stunning."

"But you don't want to look for him," she said and I hooked my arm through hers.

"Mom," I shook my head. "No. What's the point? It's a great, magical moment. It makes a good story. That's enough."

"You deserve more than a good story," she said lightly.

"Mom," I said more forcefully. "I'm twenty-two. I beat cancer twice. I've got time. Stop trying to pair me off."

"I'm not—"

"Mom," I said again. "You know I'm not into girls and you still would have pushed me at Yvette if she'd given you a chance."

She opened her mouth to object, but she started to laugh again. "I don't think I realized that."

"Let me figure out how to be happy on my own. I don't need a boy…" I trailed off. "Or a girl."

"You don't need anyone but yourself," she said. "You never have. But you'd be amazed what you can find when you have other people's support. I'm not asking you to find someone to marry. I'm not asking you to pair off. Just find some people to trust. Find your tribe. Build your village. You beat cancer twice, Annie. You deserve everything we can give you."

I blinked rapidly, pushing an elbow into her ribs. "I think we made a promise to each other to stop making the other cry," I reminded her. It had been a promise I made to her during my freshman year of college, desperate with regret when I understood how much my behavior had hurt her.

"Once you got sick, I didn't have a prayer. I'm always going to cry over you, Annie. Deal with it," she said, squeezing my arm.

"Shut up," I said. "I love you. What do you want to do?"

"Well, this is—what, day three in a row for you? What have you already done?"

"Drank a lot of beer?" I offered. She rolled her eyes. "It's been mostly eating and drinking, so I'm open."

"Why don't you recommend a beer to your dear old mom and we'll check out some of the buildings?" she suggested.

I grinned. "That's right up my alley."

• • •

I introduced her to Bent Paddle's Hopmosa, an IPA infused with orange and champagne flavors— basically a mimosa, which made it entirely acceptable as a breakfast drink. We wandered slowly through the buildings, many of which hadn't even been open when Yvette and I had been there the night before. The Eco building held my mom's attention for a while as she watched demos on state-of-the-art farming technology, things that could affect the grocery business in the future. We perused the Fine Arts Center and I fell so far in love with a painting of the Uptown Diner that my mom bought it for me.

Always a student, my mom couldn't resist the pull of the Education Building, so I followed her through until she stopped at the booth of her alma mater, grinning widely as she realized she knew the person behind it. "Text me when you're done," I muttered after introductions were made, and I wandered back towards the entrance, fanning myself.

It was hot enough outside, but the buildings were nearly unbearable. I was almost to the entrance when I heard a voice I never expected to hear again.

I felt rooted to the spot. She was standing next to entrance herself, waving a cardboard fan of Joe Mauer excessively in an attempt to cool herself. She was wearing a blue shirt with MINMIC printed on it, a stylish hijab over her hair, and she was smiling with some people I assumed were her friends.

She was older than me by about five years. I'd never seen her in person, but there wasn't a chance I'd ever forget her voice. She had saved my life.

After a moment, she walked back into the building alone and I followed her without thought. For the second time since I'd set foot in the fairgrounds, my life felt like it had been turned upside-down.

The booth she worked at was near the center of the building. My shirt stuck to my back and I was so warm that I felt uncomfortable, but I had no idea how to walk away. I approached the table, having no idea what I was going to say, until she spoke first. "Hey," she approached me. "I'm Rashida. Have you heard of MINMIC?"

I nodded, clearing my throat. Rashida. I didn't think that was the name she'd given over the phone. I remembered the name Sarah, but it hadn't been on the top of important things to keep track of at the time. "I have," I said. Nothing in her facial expression or body language changed and I realized that she probably had hundreds of calls similar to the one she'd shared with me.

"I was wondering about volunteering," I said abruptly. "If there's any way I can help."

"Oh, wow," she grinned. "Normally we have to beg. Of course. I have some pamphlets. What kind of time would you be able to commit?"

"Whatever you could use me for," I said. I felt like the words were pouring out of me with no way to stop them. I didn't think I wanted to stop them, but I was speaking without thinking, something I never did. "I just want to give back, I guess."

"Of course," she said again. It was a phrase she used frequently, including during our conversation five years prior. I tried to shake free of the memory, but it was no use.

"I don't know how to do this anymore," I said. My tone was mechanical. My words were chosen more carefully than I'd even chosen them before. "I've fought and fought and I won—I beat it. But for what? For this? It's bullshit. What's the fucking point?" I paused, but she seemed to know I wasn't done. "I don't know what to do. Can you help me?"

"Of course," she said.

And she had. She talked me down, far enough that I dumped the bottle of carefully rationed pain medication into the toilet. I had only barely retrained my right arm to listen to anything my brain asked it to do, but I made myself do it with that arm.

I had to force myself to reconnect with the present. Rashida asked me to write down my contact information and I did, standing awkwardly in place after handing it to her.

"Are there any specific things you're interested in?" she asked me.

"I don't know," I admitted. "It's all out of my comfort zone, so I don't think it matters. Give me a call if you need an extra body, I guess?"

She nodded, fanning herself again. "I want you to think about it, Annie. Even if you think you don't have the skills, there's usually something driving you to offer your time. It needs to be valuable for you, too."

"What's the most valuable to you?" I asked, biting down on the inside of my lip. I didn't know what I wanted her to say, if it mattered, but I did want to know the answer. I could hear Yvette in my head, impressed I was carrying on a conversation with a near stranger, but there was so much more going on than just that.

"Full disclosure?" she asked and I nodded. "I'm better with the one on one. Trying to talk to people about mental illness in a situation like this, when they just want to enjoy themselves, is hard for me."

"That makes sense," I nodded.

"But I try to put myself in this kind of situation as frequently as I can. The one on one is what I'm good at. This takes more work, so I learn a lot more."

"You want to challenge yourself," I acknowledged.

"I want to be able to help people in as many settings as possible," she nodded. "You never know who needs it."

I nodded, biting on the inside of my lip again. My heart was fluttering—it was too hot, I was thinking about too much that I'd worked really hard to move past.

"Can I ask you to do something for me?" I said in a rush.

"Of course," she said. "That's what I'm here for."

"Hold me to this," I said. "I'm gonna try—this is a big step for me, but don't let me tell you I'm busy. I'm not."

"Not busy," she repeated with a grin, writing it on the card I'd filled out. "Whatever's driving you, Annie, I'm glad it is. You'll be a great addition to our volunteer team. You'll be hearing directly from me."

I nodded again and I took my leave, nearly barreling my mother over. Her gaze was concerned and I couldn't blame her. The first time she'd heard of MINMIC, the Minnesota Mental Illness Coalition, was when I'd thrown how close I had become to ending my own life in her face.

I reached for her hand and she gave it. "I volunteered," I told her quietly. "Rashida, she…" I gestured over my shoulder. "She answered the phone that day. I recognized her voice."

Her grip on my hand tightened and she let me go, crossing back to the MINMIC booth and wrapping her arms around Rashida without introduction.

Rashida, for her part, seemed unaffected, like it wasn't the first time a complete stranger had hugged her like that and maybe it wasn't. She raised a hand in acknowledgement to me and I nodded again, dragging my mom from the building and out into the open.

I was gasping for air and my mom gripped my forearm as I collected myself. "I could be seventeen again," I murmured. "For as together as I feel right now."

"You never would have admitted that at seventeen," my mom said softly. "You would have run screaming from that situation. Honey, you're a lot more healed than either of want to give you credit for."

"Not feeling it right now. I need chocolate. Or a beer."

"Here we may be able to find a combo of those two things," she said teasingly, squeezing my arm again and I laughed weakly.

"There's a s'mores beer I wanted to try," I admitted, my voice less steady than I wished it was.

"Then let's find it, sweetheart. Even if it sounds disgusting," she said, trying to keep the mood light, which I appreciated. Dissecting my feelings would only make me sink further into them, and even though five years had passed, I was never ready for that, even though it was beginning to feel unavoidable.

After nearly dying during my second surgery, my entire life felt upside-down. I was sixteen years old and so angry, having felt that once was enough, but to be pulled out of school again, ripped from friends who couldn't manage my illness or my attitude, to go through chemo again, and surgery again, and almost not make it. It felt like a special kind of cruel.

I survived, but I had no one besides my mom, who was working constantly to ensure I was still covered under her medical insurance, and I was drowning in despair and no one knew.

Retraining my right arm, my dominant one, was much harder than my left had been. I had been able to go slower with my left, but I was so frustrated and so angry and when it wasn't happening when and how I wanted it to. All anyone would say to me was how lucky I was.

An angry survivor made people uncomfortable. I wasn't acting how they expected, with a gracious smile and attitude, so I was given a very large berth, and as angry and frustrated as I was, the loneliness was worse. I started even hating the word survivor, as that's all people saw me as. So I stopped trying. I withdrew, and my mom noticed, but acted like she didn't, which made me withdraw more, and I hadn't even realized I'd been rationing my meds until I had a bottle in my hands and I thought about how easily it could all be over. I was so tired, of fighting and working and of being alone. When I felt the weight of that bottle full of pills in my hand, I felt power, and a sense relief.

I didn't call MINMIC to be talked down. It was because I was certain they would never be able to. I wanted to say the words out loud I'd been thinking for months I wanted to tell someone that I should have died during the surgery—that this was the poetic ending I deserved.

But Rashida had answered the call that day. And she asked the question I knew was coming, the question I thought I had an answer for, and I didn't. She asked me why.

It took her an hour to dismantle everything I thought I understood. She figured out what I didn't realize: it all came down to my mom. At the time, I'd wished I'd died during the operation. My mom could have survived that. But if I killed myself? That would have broken her, and after everything she'd sacrificed for me, I knew I couldn't do that to her.

Understanding that didn't make me less angry or less sad. It amplified it, made me feel like a prisoner, that she was in control of every breath I took, and I held it all against her. She had no idea; she'd just gotten promoted to store manager, was around even less, but when we finally had a day together, she commented on how blessed we were, and it unhinged me. I'd had three more months to think about how angry I was, how trapped I felt, and I unleashed on her in a way I still hadn't forgiven myself for. The look on her face when I told her how I planned to die, how I couldn't even do that right, still made cameos in my dreams. In the span of a couple of minutes, I dragged her to a level of despair she hadn't felt even when I was sick.

But my mother had always been a person of action. By the end of the week, she had me in therapy. I resisted every attempt, but she would not falter, and if I thought I was more stubborn than she was, I was wrong about that.

It was the third therapist, a MINMIC therapist, who stuck. I was two weeks shy of eighteen, when she couldn't force me to do anything anymore, and I was half a year from graduation. Dr. Nelson—he insisted I call him Matt—said the thing that made the most sense out of anything anyone had said until that point.

I said next to nothing in the sessions, but he had ample info from my mom and the other two therapists who I'd eventually blown up on. He gave me my identity back.

"Why do you keep referring to yourself with your diagnosis?" he asked me.

"Because it's all anyone sees," I snapped, surprised by the question.

"You own that," he pointed out. "You don't look sick anymore, Annie." He was right. I'd regained weight. My hair was long enough to pass for a pixie cut. I was healthy.

"Where are you going to college?" he asked.

"I don't know," I said. "Community college."

His suggestion shaped my adult life. He was the one that suggested college away from home and as terrified as my mom was, she embraced it. I could be whomever I wanted outside of Willmar. I wasn't cancer survivor Annie. I was just another college freshman.

My mom refused to consider another option. She spent all of her time ensuring I would become a Gopher when I mentioned Minneapolis in passing. When she saw me looking at business management as a field of interest, it opened up the first genuine conversation we'd had in months. We both cried, I apologized for the first time, and we started to heal.

The fair was bringing out of the things I'd worked hard to forget. My mom's grip on my arm was tight, but reassuring.

"The beer's at Giggles' Campfire Grill," she said, putting her phone back in her pocket. Her gaze was warm and understanding and I pushed on my tear ducts. "Let's go."

DAY FOUR

It was noon on Sunday when my phone rang unexpectedly. My mom was the only one who ever called me, the few other people in my life understanding how much I preferred text messages, but I knew it wasn't my mom. She'd returned to Willmar early in the morning for work.

I let the call go to voicemail, rolling over in bed, but a text message came through and I groaned but grabbed it.

I know you're not busy. Call me. -Rashida

I looked at the phone in surprise. I'd pushed her and Brody and everything to the back burner to enjoy my day with my mom. Despite the heat, we had survived until sunset at the fair, eating and drinking and walking and I felt so connected to my mom that I was grateful she hadn't woken me up before she left because I didn't want to say goodbye.

But both Rashida and Brody had made appearances in my dreams. Instead of seeking them out, I'd been hiding from them, but they found me in my old hospital room where I lay in a bed next to Gwen's corpse. They accused me of lying and leading them on, then demanded I trade places with Gwen. I was having trouble shaking free of it.

I had no plans for the day and was content that way, but I'd asked Rashida to hold me accountable, so I was going to follow through.

"Annie," she said as soon as she picked up. Wherever she was, it was loud. "I knew you'd call me back."

"Funny. I didn't," I said and she laughed. "Can I help you with something?"

"I could use a volunteer," she admitted.

"When?" I asked.

"Well, now would be great."

I sat up. "Doing what?"

"I need a second body here," she told me.

"Where's here?"

"Fairgrounds, of course," she said and I snorted. I had made an intentional decision not to return to the fair for the fourth consecutive day, but once again it seemed like life had other plans for me. "I know you live nearby. I'd only need like three hours. We're down a person. What'd do you say? You'll get free entry."

I bit my lip and blew out a breath. "Okay," I said. "I'll be on my way after a shower."

"Don't bother with that," she laughed. "It's even hotter in here than it was yesterday."

"Great," I muttered. "I'll see you in a few, then."

Rashida wasn't wrong. It was well into the nineties for temperature, but the humidity was brutal. I pulled my hair into the same bun I'd worn the day before, slipped into a tank top and shorts, and walked the half mile back to the fairgrounds.

I wasn't as apprehensive as I thought. I had no idea what to expect, what would be needed from me, and normally that would be something that would terrify me, but I felt myself embracing it.

She was waiting for me at the gate near Machinery Hill, her presence enough to ensure I did not have to pay admittance for the fourth time in four days. "Part of me thought you wouldn't show," she said cheerfully.

I laughed. "That would be undeniably shitty of me. I said I would. I'm here. What's up?"

"Our mid-shift volunteer is sick," she said. "Or hungover. One of those. I just need someone else to be available to talk if needed. You won't be alone. You'll have me for a while, and a couple others will show up later. We're just short a person until three-ish."

"I don't know how much I have to offer," I pointed out.

She hesitated for a moment and I could tell she was weighing something. "You remember me too," I realized.

She stopped, reaching for my forearm, and I allowed her to lead me off the main path so we could talk. I was already sweating, my tank top sticking to my back, but I felt nothing else of note. My mom had been right about something—I would have run from this conversation before. I felt a serene sense of patience as I waited for Rashida to collect her thoughts.

"I didn't, not right away," she said. "After your mom hugged me, I knew there had to have been something, but I didn't put it together until I got home."

"I'm memorable enough after five years?" I asked in surprise. "How many similar conversations have you had?"

"Too many to count," she admitted. "It took me a long time to shake yours."

"Why?"

"I felt like I failed you," she said.

I choked on a laugh. "You saved me. Are you kidding?"

"You didn't feel that way at the time," she pointed out. "I made you hang on. I kept you alive. I didn't save you. Those are different things." She looked at me. "I knew when we hung up that you weren't going to take your life—I was absolutely certain of that—but you were more distressed than you had been when you called. It stuck with me. It changed how I talk to people. Being more miserable should have never been my goal."

"Whoa, you can only do so much," I protested. "You were not responsible for making me happy. I'm responsible for that, and I'm not good at it most of the time."

She smiled softly. "You have plenty to offer," she finally said. I took a step back in understanding. She was right; if she wanted a MINMIC success story, she'd found one. Rashida had saved my life. Matt had helped me find myself without the cancer being part of my bio.

"Thank you," I told her as we fell back into step next to each other. "For the opportunity. This, and the rest you gave me, even if you think it wasn't enough."

"It helps knowing you think it was," she said.

We walked towards the Education Building mostly in silence. I rolled my eyes at myself when I caught a yellow shirt out of the corner of my eye. Brody had the means to find me if he wanted. He hadn't taken the step, so I needed to move on. There was too much loose in my mind, things that I'd neatly filed away long ago, and letting out how I felt about Brody among that was pointless.

"Hey, you said you didn't remember me right away. What triggered that?" I asked, turning to Rashida as we entered the building.

"Well, about that," she said as we approached the MINMIC table. I took a step back in surprise when I saw who was manning it.

"Matt?" I was astonished. I hadn't talked to him since my sophomore year of college, since therapy had become less essential for me.

"Annie!" He was mostly unchanged, his dark hair graying slightly, but it had only been a couple years since I'd seen him. I gripped the hands he stretched towards me.

"I still don't understand," I admitted, looking at Rashida.

"Matt's my husband," she said and I looked at her like she was crazy. Matt had been newly married when he'd first started working with me, but I never knew it was someone else from MINMIC. There was no reason for me to know it. "I mentioned that you stopped by, a girl named Annie, and your mom hugged me... something was wiggling around in my brain about you. And he was white as a ghost as he connected all of these dots. That he didn't give up, for legality's sake. But his expression was enough for me to do a little more personal reflection."

"This is all out of control," I said, shaking my head. "How many more people can turn me inside-out like this? There's some juju on a stick here." I was muttering to myself, watching as Matt and Rashida exchanged amused glances. I looked at Matt. "I ran into Brody. Three nights ago."

He had to have re-familiarized himself with my case; I couldn't imagine he would recall Brody with such precision otherwise, but it was his turn to be surprised. "And you're still standing," he smiled. "Who woulda thought? Oh wait..." he trailed off.

"Yeah yeah," I waved him off. He had pushed me to reach out to Brody when he understood how much of my loneliness stemmed from losing him and Gwen at the same time, but I had no desire to reopen those wounds. I still didn't.

"Put me to work," I said. "It's why I'm here."

He laughed. "You asked for it."

• • •

I spent eight hours sweating through a MINMIC tee shirt, handing out pamphlets alongside Matt and Rashida and two other volunteers. Juan was a senior at the U, cute and engaging and studying sociology. Renee was Rashida's best friend, a mouthy extrovert that would have made Yvette proud.

I felt an unexpected kind of pride as I spoke with people who stopped by the table. Rashida had accurately assessed the crowd—most people did not want to talk about such deep topics while trying to enjoy a day at the fair, but plenty of people picked up pamphlets and I found myself engaging people when I didn't even need to.

I may have been the MINMIC success story, but I wasn't put on display like that was the case. It wasn't what they needed me to be. Rashida and Matt were great, sympathetic warm people who wanted nothing but to help. They were empathetic listeners, but it took me under an hour to realize how much better they were with the family of a mentally ill individual. They had both been affected by mental illness. Rashida's father died by suicide when she was a teenager and it drove her entire career. Matt had a sister with schizophrenia.

When they spoke, people listened. And as Rashida told her story, I was entranced. No one in her family had known what her father was planning, no one had suspected any kind of depression or even had an inkling that something was amiss, but when she started reading about suicide prevention, about red flags and tips, she realized the signs were everywhere, and no one knew what to look for. Her devastation was clear; he'd been gone for almost fifteen years, but her wounds were fresh.

I found myself watching Matt as she spoke and his expression was brutal. I'd obsessed over Matt's expressions for three solid years; I felt relatively good at reading them, and I knew how much he hurt for her. She blamed herself, in the same way that she blamed herself for how miserable I'd been, but those were things well beyond her control, whether she was twelve as she'd been with her father or twenty-two as she'd been with me.

Matt's story was similarly enrapturing. His older sister Lila had been his best friend when she'd starting showing symptoms in her late teens. He was the one to push his parents to bring her to a doctor, having spent weeks researching her symptoms and common disorders and digging into his family tree to determine if there were others with conditions that would help him make sense of what was happening to Lila.

His perseverance paid off. His sister was diagnosed with schizophrenia, which was a life-altering diagnosis, not just for her, but also for her family. He hadn't wanted to be right, but identifying it early was beneficial for all of them.

But as true as all of that was, it was Rashida's expressions I found myself paying attention to. After hearing her story, Matt's felt like the polar opposite. She spoke about all the things she missed while he talked about everything he saw. I didn't know Rashida much at all, but I could see how hard it was for her to know that he'd been able to see it when she hadn't been.

I spent most of the day watching them interact with others. It wasn't until Matt and Rashida left that I had an opportunity to share my own experiences.

The same girl walked past our booth three times before I got the courage to approach her. She never seemed to want to look over at us, but she always did, and there was something in her expression that felt familiar.

By all appearances, she was a well-adjusted teenager, enjoying a fair trip with her family, but there was something else beneath it that caught my attention.

I made the decision to approach her, not wait for her to approach me. She was standing in front of a booth for a local college, staring straight ahead, and I introduced myself.

I sounded unsure of myself and it bothered me, but it seemed to bolster her courage. She could have just as easily sent me away as engaged me, and I didn't know what she would do until she spoke.

"I'm Paige," she said after a moment. "Can you tell me what MINMIC does?"

"Not completely," I admitted. "This is my first shift, so I don't have all the details." Her shoulders shifted—it was a miniscule action, but one I caught, and I knew I had to keep talking. "I can't tell you everything, but I can tell you what they did for me."

She lifted her gaze to mine and I nodded once. I shed the MINMIC shirt and we went for a slow walk around the Education Building. I asked absolutely nothing of her. There wasn't anything I could provide her that would be any different if I knew what she was struggling with or not. That wasn't what I could help with. What I could give her was my personal experience. I knew our situations were probably different, very different, but I could tell her how MINMIC helped me to survive even when I hadn't been sure I'd wanted to.

The funny thing about talking to a stranger about really personal things was how easy it was. It took me years to apologize to my mom in a way that got through to her. I still hadn't figured out how to balance what I'd survived with whom I'd become, but I shared all of it anyway.

In the eyes of everyone else, my cancer automatically made my situation harder. People tried to give me a pass for my behavior, for years after they should have, so I knew it was a line to toe carefully. I didn't want Paige to think she wasn't entitled to her feelings because she was, and as I spoke of my anger and frustration and loneliness, I could see how much she could relate. Being sick had made those things worse for me, but my illness hadn't been at the core of my depression. It had taken Matt nearly a year to get me to understand that I likely would have been as lonely and angry and sad as I was if I'd never had cancer, that it was a part of my makeup no matter what else interfered.

She made her way back to her family with a MINMIC pamphlet in her pocket, and I felt more valuable than I had in my whole life.

At nine o'clock, the building closed and for the first time I could recall, I was buzzing with energy after spending the entire day around people.

Rashida and Matt headed home around six, exhausted with an early rise the next morning, and though none of us had expected it, I happily hung around with Juan and Renee until close. I wasn't completely sure there had been a sick or hungover volunteer, or if it had all been a ruse to get me out of my comfort zone, but I found if I thought about it, I didn't care all that much. It was what I'd needed for years.

Monday was my closing night at work, so I would be able to sleep in, and giving how revitalized I felt, I wasn't ready for the night to end.

Renee met up with other friends, but Juan and I decided to wander the fair together. It was his first time being on the grounds without volunteering and I couldn't stop myself from comparing his response to Eric's. He wasn't local to the Twin Cities either, but he found the kitsch of the fair endearing, a perfect sociology experiment, and I enjoyed his company.

He was also the first person I'd met in my adult life that knew I'd survived cancer. It had been discussed in his presence, Matt asking how my follow-up appointments with my oncologist had gone, and I wasn't wary about discussing it. I knew I'd probably never see Juan again, and he absorbed the information with little reaction anyway.

He was easy to talk to. His gaze was thoughtful, his hazel eyes bright, and when he asked a question, he truly seemed to want the answer. Juan's honesty made conversation easy for us. He didn't ask any questions about when I'd been sick, but even if he had, I felt like I might have answered him.

He and I were grabbing a beer when he turned to me abruptly. "What would you say if I wanted to call you, Annie?"

His question hadn't been surprising. He hadn't hid his interest, his eyes on me constantly, and he walked close enough that we bumped into each other, but I didn't mind. The attention of a cute guy was the perfect way to right my ship. "It would probably depend on what you had in mind," I admitted.

His grin was sweet and I arched onto my toes and kissed him, taking back what Brody had claimed. I was through acknowledging the flashes of yellow in my periphery like they meant anything. I hadn't realized how much I wanted to do more, to give back and engage with others until the opportunity was in front of me. I couldn't recall a time I'd felt better about myself. Focusing on the past didn't keep me in a good place   I needed to keep my focus on the future.

Juan was still smiling when I pulled back, hadn't stopped smiling even while I kissed him, and I accepted the beer he bought me, content to walk the fair beside him.

DAY FIVE

When my phone rang at nine the next morning, I officially stopped resisting. If fate wanted me at the fair every day, who was I to fight it?

Juan jolted from a deep sleep, nearly toppling out of my recliner. We'd closed down the fair, the second time for me this year, and he'd missed the last express bus of the night. I'd offered up my recliner, probably would have offered more, but he seemed in no rush to get there, and I was content to follow his lead.

I wasn't surprised to see Rashida's name flashing across my screen. "I do actually have a job," I told her when I picked up.

She laughed. "Not until three," she said. "I listen when you speak. I only need you for a couple hours. I've gotta rouse Juan from bed. He's late."

My silence was extended as I glanced over at him. His dark hair was an unruly mess, and he rose from the chair and stretched, showing off a section of his abdomen I could have spent days admiring.

Rashida started to laugh again. "Unless you know where he is," she teased.

"Shut up," I grumbled and she laughed again.

"Excellent. Matt owes me twenty bucks."

I opened my mouth to protest, but closed it. Whatever they thought had happened was likely much more than actually had. We'd kissed a couple more times, but that was it.

"I'll send him your way," I told her and she cackled again.

"Come with him," she said. "Give us a few more hours."

I shrugged. "Let me make sure that's not weird first."

She laughed again. "It won't be. I'll see you soon."

I tossed my phone on the bed beside me, eyeing Juan plainly. "Rashida?" he asked.

"You're late," I pointed out and he squinted at my microwave.

"Oh shit," he said. "Damn it. I was going to buy you breakfast. Thought I might earn some points."

I grinned. "I'd say it's the thought that counts, but you can buy me something at the fair."

"You're coming back?"

"She asked me to," I said. "And I want to. If it's not odd."

He shook his head. "No. I've got no misconceptions here. You're coming because you like the work."

"And the view," I shrugged.

He snorted and I gave in to the urge to flatten his hair. He caught my hand and smiled. "This takes a lot of work to perfect."

I rolled my eyes. "Yeah, sleeping on it is a ton of work." His grin widened and I could stop myself from laughing.

We were ready to go within a half hour, and though Rashida likely needed us given Juan's tardiness, our pace was leisurely. It had rained overnight, giving us a break from the heat.

Our conversation drifted in all directions, from personal to trivial, so when I gained the courage to ask him what drove his desire to volunteer with MINMIC, it didn't feel awkward.

"Mental illness doesn't look a specific way," he said. "The idea that people who look like they have their shit together can't possibly be affected by it frustrates me. I want people to understand that maybe I look normal. Successful."

"Hot," I added, and he chuckled.

"Maybe I look all those things, but that doesn't matter at all when I'm having a panic attack," he said. "I can look put together when I'm really not. And the most common thing I hear when I talk about it is how no one ever would have guessed… like, what does that even mean? How do we have an idea of what someone prone to anxiety would look like?"

"That's valid," I nodded, fully ready to admit I would have said something similar had he told me he suffered from anxiety if we hadn't met at a table on mental illness. I'd had the same thought about Paige the day before. "That's how I felt when I would mention how sick I was," I said, the words tumbling out.

I hadn't mentioned it to anyone as an adult, but I had three healthy years between each diagnosis. From thirteen to sixteen, when it came up, the people that didn't know me expressed their shock. At the time I took it as a compliment. I'd kicked cancer's ass. And then it came back.

"Tell me about you," he said, his voice soft. We were approaching the gate, so he got us in with his volunteer credentials, and we continued on, our pace even slower. "What drives you?"

"I don't think I know the answer to that," I admitted. "Or I'm just starting to figure it out." I shrugged. "Fighting cancer sucks. Being someone with cancer sucks. Being expected to be grateful that I survived sucks. I had no idea how to process any of that." My eyes were on the ground as we walked and I let him guide us. "I didn't have anyone besides my mom and it was hard."

"Rashida answered when you called," he said, pointing out something we both already knew, but I nodded anyway. "How old were you?"

"Seventeen," I said. "I think…" I trailed off. "I think I thought it would feel childish as I got older—

how I felt, what I said and did—but it doesn't. My feelings were real. All of them."

He was nodding and I felt like he did understand what I was saying. "How do you feel now?"

"Honestly," I said. "This is the most hopeful I've felt in my entire life." He nodded again. "I've never said any of this out loud. My best friend—the person I'm closest to, I guess—she doesn't know I was ever even sick, much less that I almost died. But for the first time, the idea of sharing that doesn't terrify me."

"You shared it with me," he pointed out.

"You're easy to talk to."

"And you don't care if I reject you," he said and I laughed.

"Maybe when you first learned about it, but I'd probably care now. But I'd do a lot of posturing to make you think I didn't," I said honestly.

"Understandable," he grinned.

"You're still buying breakfast, right?" I asked.

"Absolutely," he said.

"Okay, then we gotta run, because I know what'll score you a hell of a lot of points," I told him.

"I'm in," he said. "Lead the way."

We made it to Lulu's Public House with minutes to spare to order their breakfast juicy lulu, a breakfast sandwich featuring a sausage patty stuffed with cheese. It was what dreams were made of and when Juan took his first bite, his expression was bliss. "Damn," he said sadly. "I was resisting my crush on you," he said. "It's over now."

"Resisting? Why?" I grinned, pressing my lips to his jaw.

His hand against my hip was lazy, but his gaze was razor sharp. "Because you could eat me alive, Annie," he said matter-of-factly. "And I have this feeling I'd be more into you than you'd be into me, and that's not what I'm looking for."

"I don't know if that's true," I said slowly. "Two days ago, you're one hundred percent right, but now? I don't know."

He chuckled. "If you decide that someone is worth your time, it's not going to be me. And that's fine," he said. My thoughts drifted to Brody in his stupid yellow shirt and I bit down on my lip. "That's good for you," he pointed out.

"Juan," I said. "I just shared my sausage with you—" he snorted with laughter. "Don't underestimate me."

"Noted," he assured me and we ate and walked, picking up our speed. "Are you ready to be mercilessly teased? Because Rashida will have a field day with this," he gestured between the two of us.

"Don't worry about that," I told him as we entered the Education Building. "I play emotionless robot pretty well."

His gaze was mischievous; the building was much less busy than it had been on the weekend, and he pulled off the day-old MINMIC shirt he'd been wearing in search of a fresh one.

I was caught so off guard that I could feel my skin flush. Rashida was grinning widely and even Juan was laughing. "Touché," I held up my hands as he pulled a new blue shirt over his head. "Emotionless robot seems out of my wheelhouse, at least currently."

"I call that a good thing," he said.

"Enough flirting, lovebirds. We've got work to do," Rashida interjected, but her smile was wide.

She set me up with a fresh box of pamphlets that needed folding. Juan was on his computer, his attention singularly focused, but when he pulled out a pair of thick-framed glasses, my attention shifted to him.

Rashida definitely noticed, but she didn't tease us as much as I expected. I was more internally focused with less traffic in the building and whatever Juan was working on had all of his attention. And watching Rashida was like magic—she was so warm and open to the people who approached, even the people who question what the purpose of the table was. She was born to talk to people and I could have watched her interact with other people for days.

"One of the advocates took a call this morning," she told me during a lull. She'd been popping cough drops like they were going out of style—she seemed to always smell of eucalyptus, which made sense given all the talking she did—but it made me realize how difficult it had to be for her when her voice did give out. "From a girl named Paige."

I looked at her in surprise, feeling abruptly self-conscious. I'd intentionally said nothing about Paige. I was certain that only Renee had any idea I'd approached her. I'd left the booth the night before under the guise of needing a bathroom break. "What'd she call about?" I asked.

"She wants to talk to a counselor," she said. "Your counselor, to be frank. We set her up with Matt for this afternoon."

"Really?" I said softly. My heart was beating fast. "Is she okay?"

"She will be," Rashida smiled and squeezed my shoulder. "Your first day and you're making a difference, Annie. I hope you know how important your conversation with her was."

"I think I know better than most how important one conversation can be," I said, holding her gaze. She squeezed my shoulder again. "Thank you for telling me."

"When this is all over," she said, waving her hand around the building. "I'd love for you to come by our office. Your voice is one that could help so many people."

"I'm still figuring out how to help myself," I said, unable to take the compliment.

"I think you've come a long way on that," she pointed out. "Matt—my husband, not Matt the therapist—he could hardly believe it was you, Annie. Do you know what he said to me about you after we left? The thing that most struck him about you was how thoughtful you are, and I know what he means. You measure your words. You don't say things for a reaction. You internalize a lot, but that's created self-awareness because there's a lot you've admitted you don't want to keep in anymore." She paused while I absorbed all of that. None of it was wrong. I did think things through—to a fault sometimes—and I was introspective and self-aware. I knew what I wanted. I knew how to get those things.

"You know when things get hard and you don't feel like there's ever even an okay day?" she continued. "And I'm not even talking about when things are really bad. I just mean a long stretch of shit when you want to just throw your hands up and shout to whatever god's up there—really?!" I barked out a laugh. I knew exactly what she meant. It was how I spent most of my first year of trying hard to move out of my depression, by taking my meds and talking to Matt, and sometimes some weeks, some months, were still really hard.

I nodded. "I always made myself remember my mom," I said. "I found something worth focusing on, and I held on tight. It worked most of the time. Kept me focused on the journey instead of the minute I was in."

There was a ghost of a smile on her face and it took me a moment to place it as pride in her husband. Between the two of them, they were responsible for keeping me alive—in a lot of ways, even more responsible than the surgeons who had saved me.

"Have you had to do that lately?" she asked me. "Have you had to hunker down and find a reason to keep going lately?"

I took a moment to ponder that. My immediate response was no, but I also knew that my immediate responses tended to be whatever hurt the least to consider. She deserved my honesty, so I thought through it.

"Not exactly," I finally said. "Or, not in the same way."

"Will you tell me?" she asked.

I nodded, leaning back in the chair I was sitting in. The easiest example was one I wanted to discuss the least, but was also the most poignant given that it had already come up once. "Brody," I said. I sighed and shrugged, recognized both as defensive gestures, and I sat forward. "I feel like if I would have found him at any other point in my life—a week ago, even—it would have wrecked me. And I don't feel wrecked."

"How do you feel?" she asked

"Well, Matt—" I teased. She sounded so much like him it was uncanny. She held up her hands in surrender, but I plowed on anyway. "Nostalgic?" I said, but it came out more like a question. "I lost Gwen, and I lost him, but he didn't die, and I almost did, and… I don't know. I got mad about how easy it had to have been for him to walk away, I guess. I'd held him and Gwen at arm's length for a long time—maybe too long, but that's another problem. Blame him, blame myself? Who's at fault? Does it even matter? But I mean—self-aware, right—I was lonely. I've been lonely nearly all of my life. Seeing him would have wrecked me before, but I'm not lonely anymore." I paused for a long moment. "I still can't seem to stop thinking about him, though. It just doesn't hurt the way it used to." I nodded, more to myself than to her. "So no, I haven't had a reason to hunker down lately. I have Yvette. I signed up for a damn dating app. Maybe I'm normal now. I don't know. I'm just... better. I'm okay. And I mean it. I don't think I've ever meant it before."

It was then that I realized Juan's typing had stopped and I glanced over at him. He smiled and shrugged when he realized I'd caught him listening, but I didn't mind. The two of them had more insight into the person I'd become than anyone and I was glad to have someone to share it with.

Rashida squeezed my shoulder one more time. "It's one thing if you want to keep to yourself. I get that—I understand it, and I do not blame you for it. I don't know if I believe in fate, or god, or any of that, but I do feel, beyond anything I can explain, that I'm meant to talk to people, to share my story, and when I do it, it heals me same as it does them. Probably more me. Maybe that's not what your purpose is. Maybe there is no purpose, no divine one anyway, but if this is all we get, then what we're doing should be what makes us better, what makes the people around us better. You—god, Annie, you—made Paige better. Maybe not permanently—probably not permanently; you know it takes work, but you, with no training, with no direction, helped. Tell me that doesn't land high on your list of things that make you proud."

"It does," I admitted. "I'll come by your office when the fair is over, Rashida. We'll see where things go from there."

She wrapped an arm around me, her grip tight and reassuring. I wasn't nervous or anxious; I still felt a sense of calm I wasn't expecting, one that a part of me was still expecting to lose, but I wasn't going to fight it while I had it.

"In the meantime," Juan spoke up, his voice a little hesitant. "I don't think either of us would mind your help here until the fair is over."

"Are you kidding?" I smiled. I didn't think I believed in fate or god or a divine power either, but it seemed like I was supposed to be on the fairgrounds. I was going to be. "Breakfast juicy lulus all week long?! I'm your girl. I close at work all week; I'll be there from three to midnight-ish. I'll try to be here from nine to two."

Neither of them argued with me, something that I appreciated. I was giving a lot of time, but I found I really wanted to. Rashida pushed the box of pamphlets back in front of me and I got to work.

• • •

I'd worked retail in college, but I hadn't ever experienced anything like Roseville's back to college insanity on top of consistent small trips by fair-goers. As the executive team leader of food, and leader on duty for the evening, I was barely standing upright when the overnight team arrived.

We were a couple days away from several overnight shopping experiences for new students at the U and the nearby private schools. It was something I hadn't had any desire to participate in, something I was doubly certain of after the insanity of Monday night, but in order to schedule each of us fairly, I closed every night through Saturday, only getting my typical Thursday off. It felt like a heck of an uphill battle after the craziness of the first night.

Yvette wanted to be involved with the overnight madness and as one of the human resources leaders, it was good for her to have exposure to the overnight team, but it meant my time with her was limited when I felt like I was at my most open.

"You look different," she said, leaning against the desk as I typed up the last email I needed to send for the night. "Did you do something to your hair?"

I looked at her in surprise. I knew how different I felt, but I wasn't sure how that translated into what I looked like. I was in my Target uniform—red polo, skinny khakis, black flats, ponytail—and I was exhausted, but much more physically than mentally.

"No," I said, but I wasn't sure what else to say.

"Huh," she said. She was thrumming with energy, but it was the nervous kind. Yvette was likable, but she was young like me, and sometimes that made things hard at work. Managing a lot of tenured team members so fresh out of college was hard. She and I had both gained the trust of the dayside teams, both for completely different reasons. She did because of her warmth, because she did really want to know the nearly four hundred team members the location employed, and it was impossible to deny that once she had you one on one. For me, it was nearly the opposite. I laid out my expectations and I rewarded or corrected behavior based on how well they were met. It was my mother's style of management, though she had developed more of Yvette's people skills over the years, but it worked. No one could say they didn't know exactly what I needed from them, or that I held anyone to different standards. It made most of my work relationships very easy for me to manage.

"You're just going to have another hundred people who love you by the time this week is over, Evie," I said. "Stop bouncing."

She laughed. "Thank you for knowing what I needed to hear," she said, squeezing my shoulder as I sent my email. "How was the fair trip with your mom? What was that? Number three?" She snickered.

"Three was fine. Good," I told her. "So were four and five."

Her surprised reaction was exactly why I'd said it the way I did. I loved catching her off guard. "Don't tell me you found him," she said, her thoughts immediately, and unsurprisingly, going to Brody.

I shook my head. "I'm not looking for him."

"Then what? You were there this morning? Before work?"

I nodded, swallowing the apprehension I still felt. It wasn't the strongest emotion I was battling with, but it was still present. It wasn't that I'd lied to her— not technically. I'd never said I hadn't ever fought cancer, depression, or suicidal thoughts, and they were intensely personal things to share, but I realized I was the most worried that she wouldn't trust me anymore. I didn't want her to think that she never knew me at all when she was most of the reason I felt like all my pieces had been put back together. When I finally spoke, my words were again chosen carefully. "I feel like there's not enough time in the world to explain why. But I want to."

Her gaze was a combination of concerned and intrigued. It was probably the first time I'd expressed any kind of desire to explain something to her, but she deserved more than the half-assed friend I'd been to her. I knew I wanted to talk to her, but I didn't know how to explain the way I felt or why I felt so certain that I'd been doing things wrong for so long yet.

"Breakfast tomorrow?" she asked. "You know I won't be ready for sleep right after work."

I nodded. "Swing by my place when you're out of here," I told her.

"Will do," she told me, straightening up.

"You got this," I told her.

"I do, don't I?" she agreed, smiling.

I tugged on her long braided ponytail and watched her go. After about ten more minutes, I let my team go for the evening and I headed home, crashing as soon as my head hit the pillow.

DAY SIX

Yvette woke me from a deep sleep at quarter to eight. She'd been right when she'd claimed she wouldn't be tired—she was still nearly vibrating with energy, her eyes alight. I let her talk at me while I woke up, sharing all the sales info from the night's event, and her interactions with the team. It had gone swimmingly, as expected. She charmed everyone, including our district manager, who had made an unexpected overnight appearance to check on the event.

I dressed in a tee shirt and shorts, braided my long hair in an intentional mirror of hers, and I cleared my throat. "What's going on, Annie?" she asked softly. "You're kinda freaking me out."

I barked out a laugh. "Sorry," I said. "Will you come with me somewhere?" I asked her. "I want to—"

"Of course I will," she said, tugging on my braid. "You don't have to ask that."

I squeezed her hand and locked the door behind me and when I bypassed my car for the sidewalk, she grinned at me. "Day six?" she asked.

"Day six," I agreed.

"This must be getting expensive," she laughed.

"Not as much as you'd think," I said. We were walking at a faster pace than I had for any of my trips into the grounds. "I'm not really sure where to start," I admitted.

She gripped my hand tightly, slipping her fingers through mine. "If you think I haven't figured out that you've been through some shit, you're kidding yourself. You've also come a very long way from that first day of business college, Annie."

It had only been about four months ago, which in some ways felt crazy. It had taken so long for me and Paula to find a way to connect in college that when we finally did, there wasn't much time to build on what it could have been. Yvette and I, on the other hand, found our rhythm almost instantly. We'd ended up pairing off for some of Target's infamous mock scenarios. They were awkward and it helped us to bond quickly. She knew my management style better than anyone by the time we were done with business college and our training time in Woodbury; it was the assertive version of me that I wasn't in other situations. Her endless desire to know what makes people tick made her stick through it with me when I didn't know how to manage what it was suddenly like to have a friend. I hadn't asked for it; I'd hardly had to work for it, but it didn't make me any good at it.

I couldn't drum up the courage to say anything until we approached the gates. I handed over the credentials I'd gained to bypass the ticket lines, pulling Yvette along with me. Her eyebrows were sky high, but she didn't ask. "Let's get breakfast," I finally said. The fair in the morning smelled of sausage and eggs, the garbages mostly empty and the animals on the fair end of the fairgrounds. I was nervous, but my stomach was growling.

I ordered peanut butter and jelly French toast, Yvette stuck with an English muffin and scrambled eggs, and her gaze was nearly nothing but curious, and it gave me courage when I felt like I had nearly none.

"I'm volunteering," I said. "That's why it's day six."

"Okay," she said, sipping her orange juice. I'd ordered coffee because I needed it, but it was making me immediately jittery. "Volunteering where?"

"Have you heard of MINMIC?" I asked her, the words nearly tumbling over each other. She shook her head. "I can't decide if it makes more sense to start at the beginning or at the end and work back."

"What are you afraid of?" she asked me. "I'm not going anywhere, Annie. Like, I'm pretty sure you could confess to killing someone right now and I'd ask if you wanted help with the body."

I snorted, but it lifted some of my tension. "Honestly," I said. "I think I'm more worried about what it'll do to me to say it out loud. I've been working on that, but..." I shook my head.

"Then that's what I'm here for," she said, reaching across the table for my hand again. "You're making me nervous. Spit it out," she teased.

I squeezed my eyes shut for a moment and opened them. "Brody," I said softly. It was as good a place as anywhere to begin. "You called me out as not being honest about what had happened with him, and obviously I wasn't. I mean, he did kiss me. He was my first and last kiss. All of that was true. But he— the reason he was in my life in the first place mattered. His sister—Gwen—she was my roommate when I was twelve. We shared a hospital room for months," I squeezed my eyes shut as her grip on my hand tightened. "She was my best friend—she and Brody, they were..." I trailed off, opening my eyes, and I sighed softly. "When I was eleven, I was diagnosed with osteosarcoma—it's a type of bone cancer, and the details don't even really matter, but I had to have chemo and surgery to get rid of it, and that put me in a room with Gwen, because she had a brain tumor, and she was twelve, and... she didn't make it. And that was terrible enough—the grief and survivor's guilt and all of that, but I lost Brody too. I never saw him again, not once, since Gwen died. Until last Thursday, I guess."

"Good god, Annie," Yvette said, reaching for my other hand, which I gave without thought. "I thought you'd had a really bad break up, or... I don't know. Cancer? Are you okay now?"

I nodded, feeling nearly dizzy with relief at her response. "It's gone. I've been cancer-free since sixteen."

"Sixteen?"

I nodded again. "It came back. Had to do chemo and surgery again, but since then, I've been cancer-free."

"Jesus," she said softly. "So does this have something to do with the volunteering then?"

"Sort of," I admitted. "MINMIC is the National Alliance on Mental Illness. They provide a lot of long-term care, therapy and whatnot, which was definitely a part of my life, but... it was their short-term crisis care that really matters, at least in terms of why I'm volunteering."

She sucked in breath, but she seemed at a loss for words. I couldn't blame her. There wasn't much that could be said, so I pushed forward for her. "I think it's at the root of everything I do, I've done since... I was seventeen, a two-time cancer survivor, and I wanted nothing to do with this life anymore," I shook my head. "It took three years of therapy to feel like I had any of it under control. It took a hell of a lot longer than that for me to put any of it into use personally. I stayed afloat. That's how I lived. Until— I don't know—the last couple of months. I spent all of my time treading water and it was exhausting, it made the idea of connecting with anyone exhausting. But I think I realized—honestly, you helped me to realize—that there are more effective ways to stay above water. And I've been doing them for weeks without even being aware of it."

"Jesus," she said again, releasing my hands to push on her eyelids and I blew out a breath. Our food was dropped off and I stared at it, unsure what to do with it. "I am so sorry, Annie. I'm glad I pushed you—I still am glad—but I'm sorry if it was too much. I probably never would have done that had I known."

I nodded. "I know. So in a lot of ways, I'm glad you didn't. You asked me to be something out of my comfort zone and I was finally ready to do it. I don't talk about it with anybody because it changes what people ask of me—what they forgive me for. I needed to be held accountable, and you did that for me. I'm glad, to be honest. I don't know that I would have said that a couple days ago, but I'm saying it now."

"Shut up, Annie," she pushed on her eyelids again and I laughed.

"It's a good thing, Evie," I promised her. "I feel like a different person and you're at least partially responsible for it. At the very least you made me realize how much I don't want to be alone anymore."

She shook her head. "I don't know about that."

"I do."

"I think you might be giving credit to the wrong person," she said. "Not that I'm not grateful for it, but from what you just told me, someone else made you realize how little you wanted to be alone when you were a whole lot younger, and he's the one that's made a sudden reappearance in your life. I've been here a while, Annie. But this—you talking like this—it's a lot more recent than the past four months or so."

I shook my head, but it was her turn to speak before I could think of a counterargument. "What did you talk about?" she asked. "You and Brody?"

"That's the thing," I said. "It was all super awkward. We didn't say anything profound. We hardly said anything at all."

"He was still comfortable enough to kiss you and know you wouldn't kick his ass," she pointed out.

"Nostalgia," I shrugged. "He's not the reason I'm stronger than I was."

"No, I suppose that's true," she nodded. "You are that reason. I could have done nothing but try to pull you out of your shell, but you had to want it on your own, Annie. I hope you know that."

I nodded. "I think I do."

"I wish you'd do me a favor though," she said.

"What's that?"

"Find him, Annie," she said. "There's something itching in the back of my head about all of this. Tell me you don't feel it too."

"I don't know what I feel," I replied. "But I'm not itchy. Sometimes a moment's just a moment. Why try to make it more than that?"

"Why not?" she retorted. "Why not let something that seems magical *be* magical?"

"Because magic's not real," I told her. "Believe me, if it were, my life would have been a lot different."

She looked down for a moment, then back up at me. "I'm sorry for what you've been through. I can't imagine any of it. And—this will probably surprise you—I think positive thinking is a bunch of bullshit, but that doesn't mean you have to survive as a pessimist. You can expect more than the bare minimum. I think you're starting to realize that because you've started to expect it from yourself. He owes you an explanation, if nothing else."

"His sister died," I said. "That's the only explanation he needs."

"You loved her too," she said, shaking her head. "And you were afraid, too. You lost her, and you had to go through your own procedure, and you didn't have either of them anymore. I'm sorry she didn't make it. I'm sure his grief was unimaginable. But so was yours. Feeling selfish about that—that's allowed, Annie. That's expected."

It shouldn't have surprised me, but she hit on exactly what I struggled with so much about losing him on top of Gwen. It was the same way my mother felt about losing Alissa as a confidant. Feeling hurt by their abrupt and permanent departure from our lives felt the like the worst kind of selfish. I was still alive; I survived my surgery. But feeling bad about it sent my self-worth on a freefall. It was no one's fault, but we had so few people left, losing them was brutal for both me and my mom.

"It doesn't matter anymore," I said. "It was unnerving to run into him after all this time, but it doesn't have to be anymore than that. I don't need it to be."

"I don't think I believe you, not completely," she said. "But I'm letting it go for now."

"Thank you," I told her, glancing at my phone. "I gotta be at the booth in ten. Sorry to rush everything."

She shook her head. "Are you kidding? I'm so grateful you wanted to tell me all of this. I had no idea it was so much, Annie. I know you probably feel like you've barely been hanging on, but you've always looked more put together than that to me. Like I said, I thought you'd been burned, not…"

I squeezed her hand, unable to deny how her words filled me with pride. I wasn't someone that liked to fake it if I could help it, but it was nice to know that I looked better than I felt. The outside perspective could sometimes be the more accurate one—it took Matt a while to get that to sink in.

We finished our food and she asked to join me on my walk to the Education Building. She was contemplative, so I let her focus on her own thoughts. Mine were enough to keep me busy as well.

It was a cool, quiet morning. The Education Building traffic was at the lowest I'd seen it, so when Yvette gasped audibly, I looked at her in surprise.

Her gaze was on the MINMIC table—more specifically, at the person sitting at the MINMIC table. "Juan Rodriguez?" she said in disbelief.

He stood, mouth half open, as he looked from me to Yvette in confusion. I couldn't stop my grin. "Holy hell, Evie?" he said.

They were both frozen, staring at each other in awe, and I elbowed Yvette forward. "So you guys know each other?" I said, still grinning.

"Uh, yeah," Yvette said after a moment, finally crossing the large space to stop in front of him. I had to half jog to keep up. "Are you shitting me?" she asked him. "When did you move back here?"

"For school," he said. "I start my last year at the U next week, so three years ago?"

Yvette opened and closed her mouth, wanting to speak but she clearly had no idea where to start, and it reminded me so much of how I'd felt with Brody that it made me uncomfortable. "Juju on a stick," I muttered to myself. There were still six days to go.

"How do you know each other?" I asked, trying to push the conversation forward. They were both still awestruck in front, staring at the other, and it was unnerving .

"We both grew up in Hibbing," Yvette said. "And as the resident non-Scandinavians, we bonded."

Juan nodded, running a hand through his carefully disheveled hair. "Until I moved back to Mexico. We penpal-ed for a while, but it didn't stick. I was bad at it."

"I wasn't," Yvette pointed out.

"I know." Juan's voice was soft.

"You live here now?" she asked after a long pause. "Like permanently?"

"Until graduation at the very least," he said.

"And you volunteer for MINMIC?" she asked, though it was unnecessary. His blue shirt had MINMIC across the chest and VOLUNTEER across the back.

"Yes," he said. "I just met Annie a couple days ago."

"I kissed him," I said. It probably wasn't the right time, but it felt relevant given the way they were looking at each other.

"I would hope so," Yvette replied, not missing a beat.

"A couple of times," I added.

"Seems prudent," she agreed.

"Evie," he said, his tone desperate. "Can we—can I—"

She shook her head. "No."

"No?" Juan and I said together.

"No," she said again, but she turned to me. "I will not do anything with this unless you look for him."

My eyes felt like saucers. She was thinking about Brody? "Evie!" I exclaimed. "What the hell?"

"Are you kidding me?" she shook her head in disbelief, looking at Juan. "I haven't seen Juan in, what—six years—"

"Seven. And a half," Juan corrected her.

"Seven and a half years and the only reason I even did is because you chose today to tell me everything that's happened to you since you were a teenager. And the reason you chose today is because seeing Brody didn't undo you the way you thought, made you realize you were ready for more, and brought you to this organization in a way you wouldn't have done, not now. Not without that understanding. You have been here for six straight days. Something keeps bringing you back here, Annie!"

I shook my head. "So you're going to deny what you want because you think you know what I do?"

"Juan and I were supposed to go to prom together. Sophomore year. As friends, whatever. It wasn't what we were anymore, but we were both too afraid to say anything—" she glanced over at Juan, whose eyes were as wide as mine, but she bowled forward. "He had to go back to Mexico for a family emergency, and he never came back, and for so long all I thought was about stupid missed opportunities." She shook her head again. "You chose me, Annie. You picked me to be your friend and you should know what that means by now. I choose you, too. I'm not doing any of this without you, not when I know I'm right. Not when you have nothing to lose by trying. So just fucking do it, so I can go out with him, and we can stop pretending like we all knew so much better when we were barely kids. We don't know anything, but come on… this is all we get. This. Now. Here."

I shook my head, but I closed my eyes, and I asked myself the one question I knew she was intentionally holding back. What was I afraid of? The answer to that was easy for me to admit, but not easy in any way to face if it was true. It had been almost ten years—opening myself up to someone who had already left me behind before, understandable or not, grief-stricken or not, seemed like an easy way for me to backslide away from the progress I'd made. I'd been through hell since Gwen died, a separate, personal kind of hell that he knew nothing about, so I came with a lot of baggage, and I was terrified that he'd find reason to reject it.

I looked at Yvette, then at Juan, who was watching her, and I sighed softly. What did it matter?

I could give a couple hours to actively seek Brody out. I was stronger than I looked, than I felt.

"Fine," I said before I could talk myself out of it. "Thursday," I said. "It's my day off. He was here last Thursday. I'll give it a couple of hours."

"We all will," she said. "You don't get to half-ass this, Annie. Not happening." She leaned across the table and kissed Juan right on the mouth. It was short and to the point and I laughed despite myself. "I should've done that seven and a half years ago," she told him.

He nodded in agreement, his hazel eyes still wide. "So I can take you out?" he asked.

"After Thursday," she said. "After Annie follows through."

"I'm following through," I said. "Good god."

"I've gotta go get some sleep," she said, holding my gaze. "I'll see you tonight, Annie. Juan," she asked him for his phone number, and she shot him a text message. "After all of this—after everything— you have to set this up. Do you understand me?"

He nodded. Yvette squeezed my hand and she was gone, both of us staring after her in disbelief.

"I—" he cut himself off. "Did all of that really just happen?"

"It did," I blew out a breath. "Don't fuck it up, Juan. I'm stepping miles out of my comfort zone for this."

His smile was soft. "I know," he said. "Thank you. You guys work together?"

I nodded. "She worked her way in pretty quickly."

"I understand that," he said. "It's the same thing she did to me. Over ten years ago. This is crazy."

"Why'd you stop writing to her?" I asked curiously. The behavior reminded me at least somewhat of Brody's. I wanted to understand how

Juan could have walked away from Yvette when he clearly felt so much for her, even after so many years.

"My family was a mess," he said, shaking his head like he was trying to clear it. He looked at me for the first time since Yvette walked away. "Full-on disaster. We went back to Mexico after my grandfather died and my dad and his siblings squabbled over the estate for years. My mom hated every second we spent there. Eventually she left..." he trailed off. "It wasn't good, and I felt like I was torturing myself with what I was missing here. It was easier to live there with the life I had without the constant reminder of what I had to leave behind. It was selfish, but I was sixteen. I forgave myself for it a while ago."

I nodded along slowly. I wasn't sure how I felt about his answer, but it didn't surprise me. If he kept his word, I believed Yvette would forgive him too. Brody's reason was likely even more valid than Juan's for disappearing, but it still hurt.

"Thursday," I finally said. "Invite her to help you find Brody with you. She won't say no."

He smiled. "You're gonna look for him."

"I wouldn't have said I was if I didn't mean it," I said. "And you'll distract her from hounding me about it."

"It's the guy you were talking to Matt about, right?" He asked. "The one you ran into here after years? Just like me and Evie..." he realized.

"Yeah," I said. "He was a friend when I was sick. Could have maybe been more, but I was a baby. It doesn't matter. I'll spend a few hours seeing if I can find him and you'll get a couple extra hours with Evie. Don't blow it."

"I won't," he assured me. "But don't write it off, Annie. This is legit proof you don't have any idea what's out there. We've both been through enough, come with enough baggage… let's not write off the people who already understand that."

"Fair enough," I held up my hands in surrender. "Let's get some work done."

DAY SEVEN

I woke up exhausted on Wednesday. I'd stayed at work until nearly two, roped into event prep by Yvette, and though it was actually fun, I was wearing myself down with as little free time as I had.

After my conversations with Yvette and Juan, I revisited memories from my time in the hospital.

The kisses with Brody hadn't ever been as far buried as I pretended they were, but the moments before, the teasing and jealousy from Gwen—those were things I didn't think of often—and I was inundated with those memories.

Gwen was finally able to get her foot in the door with me the first time I met Brody. I'd been at the hospital longer than she had, but everything about her illness was more severe and more reactive than mine had been. Her treatment had been rushed and for the first couple of weeks, I felt like I only saw her at night.

Her mother Alissa never left her side. I'd seen her step-dad a handful of times, but he was always in and out, and I hadn't understood why until Brody stepped into the room one day.

Gwen had mentioned a brother. Two weeks of aggressive chemo seemed to be making everyone less nervous, and she had been prying into my business for about a week, bored out of her mind sitting in her room with a mostly silent roommate all day long. So she had mentioned him, in one of her many failed attempts to get me to talk, but when he walked in one day, about two months before he finally kissed me, I was stunned into silence.

Brody was fourteen and nearly six feet tall, so he had my attention for that reason alone, but his dark eyes and big smile captivated me. He was sweating through his Lakeville North Basketball tee shirt, fanning himself despite it being late October and freezing cold outside, and he didn't stay long. He teased Gwen for a few minutes before he left with his step-dad. He kissed Gwen on the forehead, nodded at me, and he was gone. And I was done for.

Gwen had picked up on it instantly—later I realized I probably wasn't the only girl who'd found Brody captivating—and I found myself tuning into her attempts at conversation more frequently than I had in the past. I still didn't say much, but I paid attention, and when he showed up again around dinnertime one Friday night, she figured out how to get me to open up.

Gwen and Brody's parents were finally taking a night to themselves. Alissa wasn't staying every night anymore, but Gwen seemed better, and she had pushed her mom to go home anyway. I understood that. My mom couldn't be around all the time—Willmar was three hours away and she had to keep her job, but I was jittery when she was around a lot. I preferred the freedom to feel however I wanted to without making her feel bad, and she felt bad often enough.

But because their parents were taking a night off, it meant Brody had a night on. He showed up in a thermal henley and fleece pants, popped a superhero movie in, and sprawled out between the two pullout sleeper chairs that were in the room.

"Have you seen this before?" he asked me, propping his head up on his elbow.

I shook my head, even though I had. I felt like an idiot for lying about it, but I hadn't expected him to say anything at all to me, so I'd hardly processed what he'd asked before I answered it.

"It's pretty good," he said, settling back into his pillow. "I'm Brody."

"Don't bother," Gwen said. "She doesn't say much."

I opened my mouth, then closed it. She wasn't wrong about that. There wasn't much to say.

"Okay," he shrugged, stretching out, his socked feet pushing against the edge of the sleeper he was on.

We got about halfway through the movie before I caught Gwen watching me. I had been watching Brody, watching his chest rise and fall, watching his hands, which never seemed to stop moving, and she grinned as I flushed. "Brods," she said. "Can I do your nails?"

"Yeah, sure," he said, his attention still mostly on the movie.

Gwen dug around in her bedside table and pulled out a small bag that she dumped into her lap. It had multiple colors in it and she held them up to me. "What do you think?" she asked.

Brody glanced back at me before his attention returned to the movie. The urge to engage was sudden and deep. "Blue," I said after a moment. My voice was an octave higher than normal and it was unsteady, but neither of them acted like it was anything unusual.

Gwen nodded, opening the bottle and doing a couple of her own fingernails in the midnight blue. Brody was slow to move towards her, so she focused on her own nails, and when he set his hands on the edge of her bed, she laughed. "Sorry bro, mine are wet." She looked at me. "Catch." She capped and tossed the bottle of nail polish at me before I could argue and it landed perfectly in my lap.

Brody shrugged and pivoted to my bed instead, resting his hands on the bedrail. I looked again at Gwen, who was hiding her laughter, and it irritated me enough to activate my pride. "I'm Annie," I said after a moment, sitting up straight and unscrewing the cap to the blue bottle of nail polish.

"Hi Annie," Brody said, giving me a smile similar to Gwen's, and I couldn't stop my own reluctant one in return. "I like a glittery top coat," he told me after a moment and I let out a surprised peal of laughter.

Gwen looked over at me again and I slapped a hand over my mouth before I came out of it. I lifted Brody's right hand from the rail and set it on my flannel-covered knee, biting down on my lip as I ignored the butterflies multiplying in my stomach, and I set to work. "Coming right up."

It was the type of memory that was hard to come out of, and it took me a minute to realize why. I missed Brody a lot after he disappeared from my life, but Gwen had been like a sister to me for those two months. We'd been in the same building, really no further than a room or two from each other, and when she died, I didn't feel like I had a right to react to it.

Matt was at the MINMIC table alongside Juan when I arrived on Wednesday. I was later than I promised, but less than six hours of sleep was unusual for me, and it took me longer to get out of bed than I expected.

Matt's presence didn't make my trip down memory lane any easier to manage. I spent most of my time with him processing the things I'd been through, and he'd given me the ability to wade through them without drowning, but it didn't mean it was easy all of the time.

Juan was engaging a young man at the table and I watched in earnest. He was great with people in the same way Matt and Rashida were. They were great speakers. He had personal experiences to draw on that made him even more valuable, but he didn't have to worry that he was going to choose the wrong things to say. He was good, not in an intimidating way, but I struggled to find my own voice in a situation that was likely relevant to me. My voice felt like it was wrapped around Gwen, and therefore Brody, and I couldn't help someone else until I helped myself.

"Can we go for a walk?" I asked Matt. He'd been listening to Juan as well, but my request had not surprised him.

"Of course," he said, taking Rashida's tagline. He squeezed Juan's shoulder as we passed, and I let him lead the way, having already explored most of the fair. I also knew I was a horrible decision maker when my mind was busy; I'd wander in circles without purpose.

"What's on your mind?" he asked me.

"Things we've already talked about a hundred times," I admitted.

"That's the point," he said. "We're supposed to talk about them a lot."

"Gwen," I said and he nodded, again unsurprised. "Something you said when I actually started listening to you." He chuckled, but he gestured for me to continue. "I didn't think I had a claim to the grief of losing her too. The fear of dying too—that I had, but it was like I couldn't express myself on her death without... losing myself in it."

"And running into Brody is bringing that out?"

I shrugged. "Maybe," I said. "Partially. Maybe he's the catalyst that made me realize I can think about it without falling apart."

"You've always been capable of that, Annie," he said gently.

"I don't know if that's true," I replied. "But I keep thinking about her. When I made a joke about how long it had been since I'd seen the stars, she found a way to sneak me onto the roof. It was stupid and reckless, but she started to tell me the names of the stars like she really knew them, and it took me way too long to realize she was just MinMICng them after Disney characters." I shook my head. "I still look for Mulan and Abu when I'm outside at night. I miss her."

"Of course you do," he said. "But you're managing it. So what's really under your skin right now?"

"What if he doesn't want to be found?" I asked in a rush. "What if I finally feel like a person and he says something that undoes it? What if he thinks I don't have a claim to losing Gwen too?"

"He'd be wrong," Matt replied. "And I think you know that without me having to say it. He doesn't get to claim that loss as solely his, but I don't think he would anyway."

"You don't know him," I said. "You can't say that for certain."

"There's little we can say with certainty," he said. "Annie, most people want someone to connect with when they're grieving. Most people crave empathy and understanding when processing a loss."

"I didn't have that," I said.

"I know. And I'm sorry. You were going through enough with your illness but navigating that alone had to have been painful," he touched my shoulder briefly. "What do you think you're afraid of?"

"Backsliding," I said immediately. "I'm not— things aren't as hard as they were for so long. I don't feel like I have to gasp for every breath I take. I'm terrified of going back to that."

"Do you think that Brody has the power to do that to you?"

I shook my head. "You know it's not that simple. You know my brain doesn't work like that. It's easy for me to get dark, to expect the worst, but that's better than hopeful and petrified in a lot of ways."

"What are you hoping for?" he asked. I had to fight the urge to roll my eyes at him. He was asking me questions the same way he always had, and it only irritated me because he seemed to have a point he could have made halfway through the conversation but he always made me get there myself. It could be exhausting, but I felt the familiar challenge to figure it out. He had been a nearly perfect fit for me as a therapist because he made a point to learn what motivated me and he never backed off of it.

"A connection," I admitted. It was the first time I allowed myself to consider it. "He exists in a part of my life that was one of the darkest, but he was one of the lights. Gwen's gone. I don't have her anymore, but that connection was real, and I want it back."

"Then get it, Annie," he said gently and I knew I'd landed where he'd expected me to fall. "Even if he hadn't expected anything more from those fifteen minutes than you gave him there's nothing saying you can't convince him it could be something more than that. Sometimes you have to fight for what you want. So if you want him in your life, go get him."

"That's what tomorrow is for," I told him and he laughed.

"I'd give you the time now if you want it," he said.

I shook my head. "I feel like the fair only gives when it wants to," he laughed again. "And now's not the time."

"Can I repeat something I mentioned to you in the past?"

"I don't know. Is my hour up?" I teased. "Yes."

He elbowed me teasingly. "You don't ask anything of anyone. Your expectations are so low that you can't conceive of anyone being kind to you just because. Ask more of people. Demand more. They'll only want to meet those expectations, I swear it."

"I can conceive of unexpected kindness," I said. "Because I know you and Rashida. Because I can remember it in Gwen. Because Yvette extends it on the hour." I slipped my arm through his for a moment and squeezed it tightly. "Thank you."

"That's what I'm here for," he reminded me.

"Don't bill me. I'm poor with student loans."

He snorted, shaking his head. "Honestly, when I think what I'm most proud of over the past decade or so, your progress was always near the top. I claim little responsibility—"

"Oh shut up. I'd still be in Willmar without you, hating my mom and myself. Claim the responsibility you deserve. Or I'll do it for you," I said.

He grinned at me and we stopped for a frappe before we headed back to the Education Building. He held me back for a brief moment though I'd expected it. After three years of therapy, I knew when he was done talking and when he still had more to say. Matt had more to say.

I sipped my mocha frappe while I waited for him to form his thoughts. "I know we joked about you being the MINMIC success story, but I don't want you to think that we were kidding. It's been a couple years, and I was pleased with your progress before we ended our sessions. I don't think I could have imagined that you'd end up here though. It took me until now to figure out what it is about you that's so different. You're comfortable in your own skin. You can talk about being sick. You can talk about wanting to die. And you can talk about getting past it all. Unprompted. You are remarkable. I hope you believe that."

"I'm getting there," I said, feeling more emotional than I would have expected at his assessment of me. "Can we start again?" I asked him. "Once a month or something? I think I'd feel more evened out if I knew I had someone out there who can tell if I'm not doing so well."

"Breakfast," he offered. "On your weekends off. If you want to push it into a more formal setting, we can do that, but I don't think you need me in the same way you did before. Does that work for you?"

"Sounds great," I replied, feeling some relief about not ending up back in an office setting.

"Can I put my therapist hat on for one question?"

"I'm sorry, has that been off?" I teased. "Can we start over then?" He rolled his eyes patiently. "Go ahead, Matt."

"Are you still taking the meds your psychiatrist prescribed?"

I nodded, finding that question to be the easiest one he'd asked me. "I still check in quarterly. I'm on a lower dose than I've ever been on before, but we haven't had to make any adjustments in about a year and a half."

Matt looked at me closely and I sighed softly. I hadn't been great about taking the antidepressants I'd been prescribed at seventeen; I was worse with them when therapy started to work. I felt like I didn't need them anymore, and I was quite wrong about that. Going off the medication made it way harder to go back on and I got even moodier because I hated being wrong, but eventually Dr. Ashland found something for me that worked.

"Rashida saved me once," I said. "And you did, too. Probably more than once. You made me stop blaming my mother for things so far out of her control. But Matt—the pills saved me daily. They made getting through the day a possibility— something I wouldn't have realized without you, so you should probably get that credit as well. I'm on them. I refill them. I'm happier for them."

He held my gaze for a long moment and he shook his head, chuckling to himself. "I wish you could understand how proud I am right now—you were the first case I couldn't shake. That you've come so far is really, really encouraging."

"Thank you," I said again. "Because I mostly don't feel that, but that's okay. I think anything bigger than what I'm feeling now would be too much for me. I have a best friend again. I have a job that deals primarily with people that I actually really like. I have my mom. And I think now I have MINMIC, which comes with you and Rashida and Juan."

"And then there's Brody," he said teasingly.

"Who I don't need," I pointed out.

He nodded in agreement. "That's totally true. You don't need him. But wanting him in your life— that's okay. You don't have to prove anything to anyone. Just go get what you want."

"And that's what tomorrow is for," I said. "Today, it's MINMIC and produce delivery."

• • •

I walked into work ten minutes late for my shift. About a half hour before I was planning to leave the MINMIC table, a woman in her early forties approached, uncertain. Juan was on a break and Matt was on the phone and though I knew I was capable of open conversation, I was still nervous on my own. I still felt like it would be so easy to say the wrong thing, but I bit my lip and swallowed that feeling, asking the woman how I could help her.

"I don't think I know," she admitted with a nervous laugh.

"I'm Annie," I said. "And I may not be able to help you either. But I can listen."

"You volunteer here," she said. "Why?"

"MINMIC helped me once—no, honestly, way more than that. Probably for three solid years, they helped me. I'm trying to return the favor, I guess. It was unexpected," I told her, leaning against the table. My heart was pounding. She felt like she might just walk away and I didn't want her to. "If you want to talk to the more seasoned staff, I'd be happy to find someone."

She shook her head slowly. "No. I'm sorry, I'm Linda," she said. "I don't know why I'm here. Or what I thought I'd learn about my daughter that I couldn't read on your website."

"A connection," I said after a moment and she jolted in surprise. "Someone to help you connect the dots. I can do that. If you want to tell me about her."

"How did they help you, Annie?" she asked me. "What did they do for you?"

"They saved my life," I told her honestly. "Repeatedly. I can give you more details. I can tell you everything you want to know about me—and I can tell you what I needed from my mom then—if you want to tell me a little bit more about your daughter."

She held my gaze for a moment, then looked away, before looking back at me. "I found some literature on MINMIC in my daughter's bag," she said. "Paige, she's—"

I must have reacted in surprise because Linda stopped speaking very quickly, looking at me suspiciously. I could talk to her all day about what kinds of things I would have needed, but Paige had stopped and talked to me specifically, and sharing what I knew she did felt like a very different thing. "You talked to her," Linda realized.

"The pamphlet came from me," I said after a long pause. "I can't talk to you about what we talked about. I won't do that."

"But you can tell me about you?" she asked. "You can tell me at least some of the things you shared with my daughter?"

"I can tell you my story," I said. "I can't tell you what parts of it Paige seemed to respond to because I don't know that, but even if I did, I wouldn't. But before I do any of that, I want to say one thing: seeking help is something I don't give myself credit for. I never would have approached this booth when I was going through what I went through. Your daughter is remarkably self-aware."

I shared what I had shared with Paige, what I'd also shared with Yvette and Juan, and as frequently as I'd talked about myself in the past couple of days, it never felt disingenuous or mechanical. I personalized my journey for each of the people I shared it with. With Paige, I made sure she could understand that she wasn't alone. It was how I felt at the time and it was the worst part, so I wanted her to feel like someone really understood. With her mother, I talked a lot about my relationship with my own. The way I blamed her for keeping me alive wasn't an easy thing to share and was even harder to explain, but by the time I was done, I could see some of my mother's emotions in her face. Not the devastation or the despair, but the determination to make things better, maybe even in spite of what Paige wanted.

"It's hard with teenagers, right?" I concluded. "You want her to be independent and to give her room to grow... I don't think I can speak for everyone who's been through the things I have, but I can speak for myself—I needed my mother to be my parent, not my friend. We toed a different line for a long time while I was sick..." I trailed off. "When I wasn't sick anymore, it no longer worked."

I picked up another MINMIC brochure and wrote my phone number on it. "I'm not a therapist. That is the crucial part here. But if you just want to vent or anything, please don't hesitate to call. My mom, she… it was just her and me for so long. You need support too. Please seek that out."

When Linda reached over the table and hugged me, I was shocked. It felt like I wasn't doing that much; I was sharing my story, but it hadn't been hard with her. It hadn't been hard with anyone who had no expectations of me. When she walked away, pamphlet clutched in her hand, I let out a long breath I hadn't even realized I'd been holding.

Matt and Juan had been back and observing me for a while. I turned my gaze on them. "Do I pass?" I asked teasingly.

Matt shook his head in disbelief and he hugged me too. "Every time you talk I half think my eyes and ears are playing tricks. Where's that girl who refused to say a word? Where's the one who lashed out when she couldn't stay quiet anymore?"

"Gone, I hope," I said, squeezing him back. "Speaking of, I'm going to be late for work. See you guys tomorrow."

"For the great Brody search together," Juan teased.

"I'll see you then," I said, ignoring the nerves in my belly. "You call Evie, Juan."

"Already did. She's meeting us at two."

I rolled my eyes, knowing she needed to sleep more than that, but also understanding she would resist me pushing that on her. "Whatever happens, Annie—you'll survive it," Matt reminded me.

"I know," I said. "I think I'm getting used to the idea of doing more than just surviving." I squeezed his shoulder one more time and I took off.

DAY EIGHT

I didn't get home until after three in the morning, fully aware I was trying to wear Yvette out. The night at work was mellow for me, only responsible for food instead of operations, but I sank too far into my own head. By the time Yvette and the overnight team arrived, I was ready for the distraction.

Wednesday night's event was the biggest of the four-night stretch—it was for the students from my alma mater and there were busloads of them. Yvette had the team raring to go, and I realized she even had my adrenaline pumping. I stayed well beyond when I needed to leave, engaging with the incoming freshmen, and just as the event began tapering out, exhaustion hit me hard.

Yvette was still as energetic as ever, but I knew I needed to bail. She grinned and sent me on my way and I barely hit my pillow before falling asleep.

I slept through my eight AM alarm, not rousing out of bed until there was a knock at my door. I'd slept soundly, but waking up abruptly kept the dream I'd been having fresh. It was just Gwen and me in our hospital room, but I was the adult I'd become, and she was still twelve. She was mostly silent as I begged for forgiveness, for living when she didn't, and I woke up with a sharp sense of loss.

It was Juan on the other side of my door. I let him in wordlessly, glancing at the clock. "Shit," I said, realizing it was nearly eleven o'clock. "I'm sorry."

"It's okay—Evie said you were at work late. I wasn't sure if you weren't avoiding us, and I thought I'd remind you that she won't see me unless you follow through on your promise." He grinned, running a hand through his hair.

"You're here to keep me on target," I laughed. "I'm following through! I'm just tired."

"I had to be sure," he shrugged. "I'm not letting her go again."

I nodded. He'd meant it lightly, but it made me think again that Brody may not want me involved in his life.

"I googled him," he said when I didn't say anything else.

"So did I," I admitted. "Not much out there."

He nodded. "That's true. Not much for social media. But there are some older stories, things from high school and college. Did you read any of that?"

I shook my head no, digging through my fridge for something caffeinated. I'd closed the web browser when nothing popped up for Facebook, Instagram or Snapchat, already feeling like a weird stalker, so I'd seen some sports related newspaper articles, but I hadn't read any of them.

"I can summarize if you want," he said.

"Don't make me ask," I looked at him pointedly, pouring myself a glass of cold press coffee. "Because I have too much pride to do it even if I really want to know."

He laughed. "That's basically asking."

"But not technically," I said and he laughed again.

"I guess I can tell you the basics and you can ignore me if you're not interested," he teased. I gazed at him over the mug of my iced coffee. I knew I should send him back to the fairgrounds, get in the shower, and take my designated volunteer shift, but I was still groggy, and he had me intrigued.

"Brody Washington graduated from Lakeville North High School with a four-point-oh GPA. He played basketball all four years, football for three, and got a full-ride to NDSU for football," Juan told me.

"He played wideout for a while, but was converted to a tight end late in high school and was heavily recruited by colleges before choosing North Dakota, where he had three All-American years. He double majored in economics and accounting, graduated summa cum laude, and has a job with an accounting firm in Saint Paul."

"Jesus, you got all of that from some old newspaper articles?" I asked in surprise. Not only had I felt like finding that kind of information during my own search would have been unlikely, but I was surprised by the result. The Brody I'd known when he was fourteen was interested in writing—investigative journalism. He didn't talk about it much, afraid of leaving both Gwen and me behind. Football hadn't been on his radar either, but it explained a lot about his body type. He looked more like a football player than a basketball star. I wasn't surprised by his intelligence. Brody had always been bright; I knew how little he had to focus to test well. But economics and accounting felt very foreign to me. Brody had bucked a lot of traditions—that line of work felt very traditional in a lot of ways.

Juan shook his head, pulling me out of my thoughts. "That and LinkedIn."

"He's got a LinkedIn profile? That definitely didn't pop up for me," I said, grabbing my phone off the counter.

"That's because he created it five days ago," Juan told me, raising his eyebrows.

"That doesn't mean anything," I shrugged.

"Get any profile views lately?"

"I refuse to look at that," I shook my head.

"I refuse your refusal," he countered. "Look at it, Annie."

I rolled my eyes but I opened the app on my phone, noting two new connection requests from college classmates, and four new profile views, two of which were anonymous. I shrugged and handed Juan my phone.

"It's him," he said.

"Maybe," I allowed. "There's no way to know that for sure, and there's no point in thinking all that hard about it."

He smiled, handing me my phone back. "I'm going to shower and I'll head towards the fairgrounds. You can head back."

"Do you care if I wait for you?" he asked.

"Juan," I rolled my eyes again. "I'm not lying. I'm coming."

"I know," he shrugged. "But I think you're more nervous than you're acting, and I want you to know you've got someone on your side."

"You're on your own side," I teased.

"Even if I thought Evie was being honest about staying away from me," he grinned, "This isn't her call, it's yours. You don't have to do anything you don't want to, and I think you're nervous, Annie. I'm trying to be stoically available if you need it."

"I'm okay," I said, happy to realize that I meant it. Juan's kindness also filled me with a sense of happiness I hadn't expected. "But stick around if you want. There's more coffee in the fridge. I'll be out in a few."

I tried to categorize my emotions as I washed my hair. I didn't feel the nerves I'd felt the night before and I didn't trust it—feeling at ease about searching for Brody, especially after my dream about Gwen, felt unrealistic. I was waiting for the other shoe to drop.

I'd revisited several memories of Brody as I culled through the produce at work the night before. Normally I would shut it down before I let my thoughts go too far, but I stopped resisting, and the recollection wound up feeling more nostalgic than painful.

There were two memories that stuck with me. The first was before our first kiss, when he and I were still trying to figure out what we were to each other. We'd become really good friends, but there was more there, more to explore, and neither of us had any idea how to do it.

It was a while after the movie night. We were watching a video on his phone, something stupid about dogs that he knew I'd find funnier than he would. We were both sitting on my bed, his right side pressed against my left, and my skin felt like it was singing everywhere we were touching.

The French bulldog was adorable in the video, but all I could think of was how close he was to me. He smelled like teenage boy, like sweat and deodorant and whatever meal he ate last, and I couldn't get enough.

My mom had walked in with his abruptly, giving us no time to react. I shied away from him, but I realized immediately that he hadn't moved, hadn't given me any additional space, so I inched back towards him, holding in my happy sigh when our arms pressed together again.

"We gotta go, Brods," Alissa had said to Brody at the time.

"Video's almost over, Mom," he'd said, not lifting his eyes from the screen. He shifted the phone from his right hand to his left, his right hand falling to the nearly nonexistent space between us. Emboldened by his move, I hooked my pinky around his, holding my breath until he returned the pressure, sighing softly.

It had been the first time I felt with any certainty that he liked me too. He paid a lot of attention to me, but Brody was a genuinely nice boy, so that alone wasn't enough for me to believe I wasn't making it all up in my head. That returned action, the tightening of his finger around mine, was what eventually made me confident enough to kiss him.

In the second memory, we were alone for the first time. It was also the last; it was the week after our first kiss, the week before Gwen would die during surgery.

It was the first time I'd ever touched anyone in a way that wasn't solely friendly. Our hands were tentative and innocent, only getting the courage to explore a couple inches of abdomen. I could still remember how intense it was; I realized much later it was my first experience with lust.

As memorable as that was, it wasn't why I'd avoided the memory so much in the past. Brody knew as well as I did that we weren't likely to get the kind of alone time we had again, so he'd had one rule. It was something he told me when he carefully pushed my hospital bed towards the window. He wasn't making eye contact, his attention on the cords and lines to avoid unhooking anything that would catch the attention of the nurses on duty.

"For tonight," he'd said. "You're not sick. Gwen's not sick. We're lying in my bedroom. We're normal teenagers. Can wc do that?"

I nodded breathlessly. He climbed into the bed besides me, looking out the window over his head. "This is what my room's like," he'd said. "My bed is pushed right up to the window like this so I can look at the stars if I want to."

I laid beside him, our arms pressed together, and I looked out the window with him. The lights from the parking lot were too bright to make out anything in the sky, but I would have stayed there with him forever.

"There's probably a couple of socks on the floor," he said. "I would have tried to pick them up for you, but I would have missed a couple. Makes my mom nuts." He glanced over at me, his fingers slipping through mine. "The TV is on, for background noise, not because we're watching it. Just my bedside lamp would be on, so it's dim, and I'd probably pretend to be very interested in the stars when all I'd want to do is look at you."

I'd blushed at the time, but rolled over and kissed him. Our hands explored then, but it was the conversation that riveted me. No one talked to me like Brody did. Everything was so honest and open-ended; I felt like we could have built something great on that friendship.

It was when he told me he was interested in writing, when he talked about the things that made him happy—his family, volunteering with his church, karaoke with his friends—that hooked me.

I found myself reciprocating his honesty because he had so much of it. I told him that my mother had made me interested in the grocery business and sales, though I never would have admitted it to her at the time. I talked about the music I listened to when I was alone and how it had been my saving grace before he and Gwen had worked their way in. I shared something with him I hadn't told a single person before or since, not Matt during therapy or my mom at any point in our relationship. I told him that I spent a lot of time rewriting my story in my head—that I was in the hospital for exhaustion because I led a really awesome girl metal band and I just needed some recuperation.

His response had been instantaneous, not sad or pitying, and I held onto it for months after Gwen was gone. "What do you play?"

"Bass guitar," I answered immediately. "And I sing backup."

I was flat on my back at that point, but he was lying on his side, his hand under my shirt, pressed against my bare stomach, and he laughed, but he wasn't teasing me. He liked the story. "Do I factor into your metal world?"

"Oh yeah," I grinned. "Metal girl and hip hop guy? We're like star-crossed lovers with a great collaboration opportunity. I've had hours to write our story, Brody."

He'd smiled and kissed my temple, and it had been a moment I buried out of anger months later. Writing that story in my head made it really hard to let go of him when he seemed to have no issue doing the same thing to me. I buried it, and though the moments when it had tried to come out were rare, I normally felt like I could hyperventilate if I spent any time processing it.

My shower was long, but Juan was waiting patiently when I emerged. I dressed comfortably, knowing I'd be at the MINMIC table for at least a couple of hours. It was also the most humid day since I'd gone to the fair with my mother.

Juan was quietly contemplative beside me as we headed towards the fairgrounds. I didn't push him, but it took him longer than I expected to say what was on his mind.

"What was he like?" Juan asked. "Brody."

"He was thoughtful," I told him. "If I had to give him one descriptive word, that would be it. He always seemed more mature than he had any reason to be, even given Gwen. He cared about other people, about how what he said would affect them, so his words were measured and meaningful." I glanced over at Juan for a moment. "He was the opposite of me in a lot of ways. I was intentionally brash, and I only got better at that after Gwen died and I got sick again. I sought out ways to hurt people. I think I've got a better than average group of great people in my life, but his kindness was pretty unparalleled."

"Sometimes I wonder what people would say about me if they were asked," he said as an explanation for his question. "You've had one conversation with him in nearly ten years and you had a lot of anger towards him for a while, and still your first words are kind ones. I don't think you're as different from him as you think you are."

"If you want to know what Evie thought about you for the last seven years, ask her. She'll tell you the truth," I said teasingly.

"I know," he shrugged. "Sometimes the truth hurts."

"Most of the time," I amended and he laughed. "Coming from a near stranger, Juan—you remind me of him in some ways. You are empathetic and attentive—you want to make the people around you better. I don't know a lot of people who are better at it than you are."

"You," he said and I shook my head in disagreement. "I'm serious," he pressed. "The way you talked to Paige's mom. How thankful you are with Matt and Rashida and Evie. I know you don't want to think it, but you—you're good at this. You could be great at this."

I waved him off. "I don't want all that," I admitted. "I want to help people—I do want that. But I also—I'm happy doing what I'm doing. I don't want to burn out. I want to keep produce fresh and manage a team and… honestly, do the stuff I'm doing at Target. Maybe it seems stupid and trivial compared to all of the things MINMIC is capable of, but if someone's gotta keep bananas the appropriate shade of yellow and green, I'm good being that person," I admitted. "And I want to learn how Rashida talked me down. I want that skill, maybe more than I've wanted anything."

"We'll make sure you get it," he assured me. "The crisis phone scares the shit out of me," he admitted after a long moment. "I'm better in person, when I have time to build a rapport, and the entire time I'm on the phone, all I can think is that I'm going to say the wrong thing and they're going to hang up and I won't have done enough to convince them that life is worth living."

I nodded slowly. I could understand that fear, but I didn't feel it myself. I hadn't had a conversation yet where I felt like I needed to fear for someone's life, but I had been there myself, and that understanding would help me reach people. I believed that to my core. "You know what Rashida would suggest," I pointed out.

"Yeah," he agreed. "Do it more often. Expose myself to it more often."

"Just like she does at the table," I nodded. "I don't think she's wrong about that."

"I don't either," he admitted. "But it still scares me."

"It's good to know what you're afraid of," I replied. "Better than letting it sneak up on you."

"Are you afraid of today?" he asked. "Of finding Brody. Or not finding Brody."

I shook my head. "I've never been a take-things-as-they-come-kinda-girl, but that's how I'm feeling right now. This week at the fair has felt entirely out of my control, like something else is at work, and I've never felt that a day in my life until now. I'm going with it. Maybe I'll find him. Maybe I won't. Maybe it won't matter. It's just another day, Juan."

• • •

I felt the most dialed in at the MINMIC booth as I had felt the entire week at the fair. The Education Building was sweltering by noon, a breezeless sauna in the heat and humidity, but my focus was sharp and my engagement was high. Rashida was more than happy to let me talk to people as they approached, and by the time my volunteer shift ended at two, my blood was pumping.

Yvette arrived exactly on time, running on very little sleep but looking radiant. Her dark hair was in a high ponytail and she dressed as relaxed as I had in shorts and a tank top and by the grace of some god, she wasn't sweating.

She made no comment about my appearance, which left me to think I was either beyond all hope, or I didn't look as gross as I felt. I slipped out of my MINMIC shirt to the tank top I had underneath while Yvette laid out the plan.

"First and foremost," she said. "Matt and Rashida—you stay here and save people." I snorted, but Juan looked at her in awe. She was singularly focused on finding Brody—much more than I was—but she knew how important MINMIC was. She wasn't going to ask them to help.

"We can do that," Rashida grinned.

"Annie, you and I are going—"

"Oh hell no," I interrupted her. "You and I are going nowhere. You are taking this handsome man with you." I gestured at Juan.

She shook her head. "No way. You'll bail."

"I won't," I said. "I promised you I'd look for him and I will, but I'm doing it alone. I'm hungry. I'm going to grab something from the Food Building. I'll start there. All the stands in yellow, I'll scope them out. I'll ask about him if I feel comfortable doing it. You can do exactly the same thing, but you're doing it with Juan."

"I—"

"Okay," Juan interjected gently. "She's not bailing, Evie. She's doing this half for us anyway. Let her have this."

"Like you're unbiased," she grumbled, but I knew she was going to cave.

"Of course I'm not," he grinned. "I want to spend this day with you. Tell me you don't want me to and we can all split up and look for him."

She held his gaze for a moment. "You'd look for him too? Alone?" He shrugged, suddenly self-conscious, and I hid my smile. "Goddamnit," she grumbled again. She kissed him briefly and I burst out laughing. "Shut up, Annie."

"Nope," I said. "I'm getting a wild rice cheeseburger. I'm going to go melt my face off some more in the Food Building. You have my number. Text me if you find him."

"Check in with me," Yvette said and her voice was softer. I knew she didn't want to push me harder than I was ready to be pushed, but I felt fine. I squeezed her hand once, shared a glance with Juan, and I left them behind.

• • •

If I thought the Education Building was a sauna, it had nothing on the Food Building. It had to be well over one hundred degrees and as I watched the poor guys behind the wild rice burger stand in their plastic tarps and splatter masks, I realized how lucky I'd been to volunteer in a building without dozens of ovens and fryers.

I brought my burger outside to enjoy, but I'd catalogued some of the stands with yellow shirts, and I realized there were a lot more than I first thought. I hadn't stopped acknowledging the yellow in my periphery, try as I might, but I also hadn't spent any time connecting the shirts with the brands on them. There were quite a few and as I finished my burger, I realized for the first time that the task ahead of me was daunting. I also forced myself to acknowledge that there would be some disappointment if I didn't find him.

Liquid courage felt like it would be beneficial, so I crossed the courtyard to the Agriculture Building and bought a beer flight from the Brewer's Association. I picked the two I liked the best and I sipped them slowly, but I slammed the final two, rising to my feet and heading back into the Food Building before I could talk myself out of it.

It was so hot, which wasn't making anyone happier. I gave myself a goal and I stuck to it. If a line was short or didn't exist and the staff wore yellow, I'd ask about him. If the booth was busy, I'd take a peek but move on. Even so, it took me nearly an hour to get through the building, and though I hadn't talked to someone at every booth, I felt confident that Brody didn't work at any of the stands inside.

I still wasn't sure what I was seeking. Did I want a continuation of what we'd had ten years prior? Did I want closure? A connection seemed the most likely answer given how I felt about Yvette, but I couldn't land on that completely. I felt like I was looking for a combination of all of those things, which had me worried that I was setting myself up for disappointment.

I didn't know where I was headed next. I needed to connect with Yvette and Juan, see where they had already been, so I pulled my phone from my pocket and walked directly into someone I'd seen before. I walked directly into Sue.

I was speechless, shaking my head in disbelief. It felt like the fair was acting again, and when she spoke, I had to fight the urge to laugh.

"Annie, right?" She asked, gripping my forearms to straighten herself from our collision. She didn't wait for a response. "I've been thinking about you."

"Hi," I said, unable to think of anything else to say in return.

"I didn't think I'd see you again. Did you ever find your boy?"

I shook my head. "I'm looking for him now."

"Really?" she raised her eyebrows in surprise. "I didn't expect you'd give in on that."

"Evie—the girl I was with before—she can be convincing," I said.

Sue laughed. "I believe that. Where have you been so far?"

"Food Building," I said. "Evie's out there looking too."

She nodded. "I've been thinking about you," she repeated. "And I think I've come up with a solid list of most of the vendors in yellow. If you want it."

I looked at her in surprise.

"It's a good story, the little I know," she said. "And if I'm being honest, your reaction to me claiming you couldn't have been through anything bad hit me hard. I don't know you. It was a crappy judgment to make."

I shrugged. "You're not the first to make it," I admitted. "But I don't want to get buried in all of that. If you have a list, mental or otherwise, I'm happy to take it."

"I can write it down," she said. "Come with me."

I nodded and followed her, walking in step beside her. "What's your story, Sue?" I asked. "Twenty-five years here. What's that like?"

"I love it," she said. "I decided a long time ago that I wasn't going to spend time doing things I don't love. I'm a teacher—special ed at a middle school for the same twenty-five years—and I love that too.

Being here gets me ready for the school year. It's a tradition and it suddenly felt like I'd be jinxing my whole year if I didn't come back. You know?" We stopped at a fair information booth and she let herself inside it, grabbing a pen and a state fair map.

"I've been here every day this year," I admitted. "So that I definitely get."

She laughed, turning her attention to the paper in front of her. She wrote quickly, but neatly, talking to herself a little as she came up with a list that was rapidly becoming intimidating. It was getting more and more humid, the sun gratefully disappearing behind clouds, but it was one of those days that made being outside exhausting. Even with the extra sleep I'd gotten, I knew I was going to tire easily.

"I'm sorry," she told me and I refocused my attention on her. "I'm normally one of the best at not making assumptions about people, but I did with you."

"We all do it," I shrugged. "No big deal."

"Whatever it was," she said carefully. "It's better now?"

I contemplated that. I was cancer-free, but that hadn't been the hardest thing I'd been through, not by a long shot. Still, I knew I was healing in a way I wouldn't have acknowledged before. "Yes," I said simply.

"I'm glad to hear that," she said, handing me her overwhelmingly long list. "I hope he's worth all of this."

"So do I," I smiled. "Thank you, Sue. Take care of yourself."

"You too, Annie. Good luck. Come find me if you do find him. I'd love to hear how this ends."

"I will," I said, and I meant it. I gave her a final wave and looked down at my list, knowing I was going to need something to drink to keep going.

I took a photo of the list and sent it to Yvette, who reported no luck at all of the fair's Pronto Pup stands. I suggested we divide the list by area. I would start by the cattle barns and she and Juan could hit up Machinery Hill and we could meet in the middle. The list was just about twenty stands, so I let that overwhelm me before I stopped for lemonade, checking in on that stand's yellow shirted employee before making the walk towards the barns.

My feet were aching by the third booth. I'd barely made it to the Midway when I felt with certainty that I wasn't going to find him. The disappointment washed over me, but it was bearable. It was a connection I was seeking, and not knowing what could have been still ate at me, but it was okay. I stopped for water, committing to check the Midway booths before calling it, when my phone rang.

I normally didn't answer phone calls from numbers I didn't know, but I still felt like a lot about the fair was happening outside of my control. Maybe I wasn't going to find Brody, but there were still other things at play worth acknowledging.

Given that, I wasn't all that surprised to hear Linda, Paige's mom, on the other side of the call. The fairgrounds were loud, but I could hear the panic in her tone, and it grounded me in a way that I both hadn't expected and was grateful for.

"Linda, I'm going to call you right back," I said. "I can't hear anything where I'm at. Give me five minutes to find a quiet place, okay?"

"Okay," she said and I hung up, even though I was partially afraid she wouldn't answer when I called back. I'd spent a week on the grounds; I knew a couple of quiet places, so I headed out of the Midway and towards the Horse Barn. The west side of the barn was mostly empty and I felt like I'd have half a shot at being able to have the conversation with her that she wanted to have.

Biting my lip, I glanced at the list in my hand. I knew what it meant if I put it away, but it was the right thing to do. I folded it up and slipped it into my back pocket, pulling my phone out to return Linda's call.

DAY NINE

I awoke disoriented on Friday, my mind fuzzy and my body sore. After my conversation with Linda, which had lasted a better part of an hour, I'd barely left the Horse Barn before the sky broke open.

I'd been soaked in seconds and I knew it was over. Talking with Linda had drained me of any mental energy I'd had in the beginning of the day. She was so worried about Paige, so nervous that her daughter still hadn't said anything to her, that I knew she was prying for more information from me. I didn't have much to share either way, but I wasn't going to break the privacy I'd had with Paige. When we hung up, I felt like I had talked Linda down, that she wasn't going to knock down her daughter's bedroom door and demand answers, but I also felt like it would be a reoccurring kind of call.

I'd ducked into Coasters to send Yvette a message. I didn't say anything about being done with the search, or whether I'd been successful or not. All I did was tell her I was going to Uber home and I left.

I didn't Uber though. I knew the line would be long and I'd end up just as soaked, so I walked the half mile home in the pouring rain. When I got there, I stripped down in the bathroom, took a short, steaming soak in the tub and passed out on my bed by eight.

As soon as I woke up, I knew I could have slept longer, so I glanced around in confusion until I heard another knock at my door. It was about seven, which was way earlier than any of the MINMIC folks had checked on me before, so I assumed it had to be Yvette, wanting details on my failed search for Brody.

I was wrong. It was my mom, holding a bag of what smelled like cinnamon rolls. I looked at her in surprise. "Mom," I said. "I've been answering you."

I had been. We'd been texting most of the week, but we were both busy between work and other obligations. I hadn't said anything about my search for Brody, not wanting to give her any reason to worry.

I stepped back to allow her inside. "For the record, I did try to call this time. Your phone is dead," she said. The pieces of my phone were in bags of rice on my counter. After the downpour at the fair, my phone had gotten wet enough to be worrisome. I gestured at it before powering up my Keurig. "It's my weekend off with Margie," my mom added.

"Oh yeah," I said, rubbing my eyes. I dug a pair of shorts out of my dresser, slipping them on under the long tee shirt I had on. I was still very groggy, my mind unfocused. I hadn't spent much time considering my mom's weekend plans.

Since becoming a store manager in Willmar, she'd made a couple great friends at other regionally located Cub Foods. They each had the same insane schedule, so no one else had hurt feelings when plans fell through. Margie was my favorite of those friends. She was single, like my mom, had a couple adult kids a little older than me, and she made my mom have the fun she didn't seek out on her own. If I remembered correctly, they were heading to Treasure Island for some gambling, a show, and to drink too much wine and laugh a lot. It always rejuvenated her to be able to herself for a weekend, not a mom or a boss or anything other than what she wanted to be.

"How's the MINMIC volunteering going?" she asked, dishing up the cinnamon rolls.

"It's good. Cathartic in some ways," I said, but I'd already told her that via text. There was a part that

I hadn't. "I set up recurring time with Matt. Twice a month."

She looked alarmed, but it faded quickly. I never sought it out on my own before. It was something new, but something good. "You don't want to lose the progress you feel like you made," she said in realization.

I shrugged and nodded. "Yeah. I feel—I don't know—like an adult is supposed to? It's odd."

She laughed, but it sounded somewhat hollow. My attention zeroed in on her, the grogginess lifting. "What's up, Mom?"

She pushed the mug of coffee I'd brewed at me, sighing softly. I took a sip as I waited for her to collect her thoughts, but the butterflies that were rapidly multiplying in my stomach made me feel nauseous. There was something about her posture, about how she struggled to maintain eye contact, that made me really nervous.

"Last week," she said slowly. "When I was here… I wasn't here completely to check on you. I had an appointment."

I swallowed hard. "What kind of appointment, Mom?"

She tore her gaze from me and I could see how hard she was battling and I knew why. She was afraid that whatever she was about to say to me would send me on that downward spiral I was terrified of. And as scared as I was, she wanted to hear me tell her I wouldn't. I was going to tell her that, even if I wasn't sure of it at all.

"Mom," I said again. "I'm grown. I'm managing. I need you to tell me and know I'm not who I was at seventeen. Eighteen. Last month. You're scaring me. I am afraid, but I want to help. Please."

She brought a hand to her mouth, straightening, and she reached for me with her other hand. I held on tight. "I found a lump," she said, biting down on her lip. My stomach rose to my throat and plummeted back down and I only kept my nausea at bay by squeezing her hand so tightly I was sure it had to hurt. "On my right breast. And last Friday, I had a biopsy."

"You got the results," I said in understanding. She nodded, taking in a shaky breath. "Fuck," I swore loudly. She didn't chastise me, probably for the first time ever, and I knew that the lump had been cancerous. "Fuck," I said again. I could feel the fear and the rage and the unfairness of it all, how easily it could swallow me, but I stuffed it as far down as I could manage. It wasn't far enough—it wasn't going to last—but I could be knowledge seeking while I put all of the pieces together. The rest I could process later.

"How bad?" I asked, squeezing my eyes shut.

"We did some scans and tests yesterday," she replied. "Stage Two. Tumor in my right, cancerous cells in my left. It hasn't spread. I start treatment next week."

"Mom," I said helplessly. "What kind of treatment? What's the plan?"

"Chemo," she said. "Then surgery."

I let out a bark of a laugh. "Are you kidding?" I laughed again. "Goddamnit," I could feel the tears behind my eyes. "I'm so sorry. I'm—this is not helping."

"Honey, you having a real reaction—that helps," she said, releasing my hands to wipe her own tears. "It should be just a handful of chemo rounds, and then I'm going to have both breasts removed. It's not worth risking it returning, and it's not like they're being used for anything," she cracked.

"Mom," I chastised her, but I shook my head. "How does this happen? How does this keep happening to us?"

"You wouldn't believe how many times I've thought the same thing in the past week," she admitted, wiping her cheeks again. "I'm sorry I waited to tell you. I should have—"

I shook my head. "You did what you needed to for you. If anyone can understand that, it's me," I pointed out. "I'm angry. And afraid. But none of it's your fault. I have a hold on it. I don't want to be a liability anymore. I don't want you to have to worry about how what you say will affect me."

"Honey, I'm your mother. I always have to worry about that," she said.

I shook my head. I was losing focus, the fear creeping up again. There was no way I'd survive losing her. I had survived nearly everything else; I'd survived wanting to die because I'd understood how much it would devastate her if I was gone. What would I do without her grounding me in that?

"I'll take today off," I told her. "I can give you whatever you need from me."

"Annie," she said. "I want this weekend with Margie. I want a weekend where I feel normal before I'm not anymore. There's so much I didn't understand about how you felt about having cancer that I feel like I'm going to understand with clarity—I want a few more days of not having to feel that way. Is that selfish?"

"Yes," I told her. "And thank god for it." It broke the dam on the tears I was holding in. I didn't cry often, hardly ever as an adult, but the only one who could bring it out in me was my mom. "You've never been selfish a day in your life," I said, brushing the tears off my cheeks. "If being normal is what you want, it's what you get while you can have it."

She wrapped her arms around me and I cried on her shoulder, eventually pinching the bridge of my nose hard to make myself stop. I was going to fall apart—there seemed no way around it—but if I did it in front of her, she'd never do what she wanted. I wanted her to stay; I wanted my mom with me before she had to face chemo, something I had considerably more experience with than she had, had always downplayed how it had made me feel. Every single thing she was about to go through she would compare to my own journey and I knew she would struggle with the pain more than anything, and not because it hurt her, but because of how much I'd bore silently.

"When do you have to meet Margie?" I asked her.

"Check-in isn't until three," she said.

"Will you stay with me until then?" I asked her.

Her tears started back up then and I hugged her again. "Of course."

• • •

We spent the day watching daytime TV, the same stuff we'd watched when I was sick—the *Price is Right*, *Young and the Restless*—and we ate all four cinnamon rolls, sitting on my bed with our backs against the wall.

I called Rashida to let her know I'd had a family emergency and wouldn't be able to make it to the MINMIC booth that day. She asked me for details, but I wasn't ready to provide them. I realized it was the first day since the fair had opened that I wasn't going to be there.

I didn't cry again, but my mom did. I told her about Brody, that I'd tried to find him and failed, and that I was disappointed by it. We talked about Gwen, about the brave, self-sacrificing girl the world had lost way too early. She admitted to me something I already assumed but that she had never said out loud—how grateful she was that it was Gwen instead of me. She knew how horrible the thought was; she knew she would have hated Alissa's guts if the situation had been reversed and I'd died instead of Gwen, but she still felt it.

Anyone else would have thought I was crazy for going into work after learning her mom had cancer, but my mom completely understood it. It was my leader on duty night—once I let that out, she wouldn't think of me not going. I had a responsibility to the team that I managed. Life didn't stop for anything, or anyone. Not even her.

I knew sitting at home would likely make me insane with worry anyway. If anything was likely to make me sink into my head and lose all the progress I'd made, it was being alone.

My mom stuck around while I showered, asking to French braid my long hair while it was drying. It was something that she hadn't done since before I got sick the first time—it had been that long since my hair was lengthy enough to do it. A sob got caught in my throat and I could feel myself unraveling, but I nodded, trying to weave my emotions back together while she did the same with my hair.

I was going to be late to work again; she was going to be late to meeting Margie, but neither of us wanted to leave the other behind. I knew it had to be me. I had to rip off the bandage because she was still trying to take care of me.

"I'd say maybe don't gamble too much," I said teasingly as I hugged her tightly for the umpteenth time. "Our luck seems catastrophically bad."

"Good call," she said into my shoulder. She smoothed my hair down. "I'll be back on Monday evening. My first appointment is Tuesday morning."

"I'll be there," I told her, pushing on my eyelids again. I normally wore mascara, but I'd smartly decided to skip it, and I knew it was a good choice. "Whatever you need, Mom. Now go—have fun. But tell Margie before you leave. She deserves to know, too. You know she'll be a warrior for you, just like you were for me."

"I love you," she told me, kissing my forehead.

"I love you too," I said, and I watched her go for only a moment before I grabbed my keys and headed to work.

• • •

Keeping my mind as empty as I needed to wasn't working as leader on duty. I needed something more monotonous. The constant guest interaction and team member needs were making it hard for me to separate my emotions.

Once my mom was out of my line of sight, I had burst into such torrential tears, I didn't think I'd be able to collect myself. The fear was the worst. I could do absolutely nothing about what was happening to her, and my own experience with cancer didn't reassure me at all. I couldn't embrace the anger in its place, not if I was going to be an effective manager at work, so it left the third strongest of the emotions—a sort of indignant despair.

I wasn't myself. I was disengaged and though I'd spent a lot of time masking that as a teen, I hadn't ever had to at work, and it was hard.

I kept reverting to me at eleven, when I was tired all the time, kept spiking fevers, and no one knew why. I'd seen so many doctors, my mom trading shifts at work all the time so we could see someone new. She refused to buy that it was just typical hormones, that puberty was hitting me and that it was the best explanation for my exhaustion. It could have played a part to be sure, but it didn't explain my constant high temperature, or the body aches I couldn't manage.

She got an appointment with an endocrinologist out of sheer force of will. It took a few weeks to get into see her, but she immediately sent me off for scans. It took a couple to find the tumor in my arm, something that they hadn't been looking for. At eleven, I understand that tumors weren't good, that cancer was bad, but I didn't know anything more than that.

The doctor told my mom first. My mom, I learned later, had already suspected something like cancer, and the first emotion she felt at my diagnosis was relief. She didn't tell me that until therapy started to work. I tried to imagine her telling me it before then and I knew it would have gone horribly awry had she tried. I never would have understood it until I came to terms with it myself, but having a diagnosis meant we could finally fight it.

I didn't know what to expect from chemo until I had it, and if I thought I knew what it meant to be exhausted, I didn't have a clue. It made me vomit, it took my hair, it made me feel worse than the cancer ever did. It took Matt a really long time to get me to admit it, but a lot of my resentment was tied up in how painful treatment was. I'd buried it for the sake of my mother's feelings. She owned so much that I faked it as much as I could.

Knowing she was about to be exposed to that made me sick. It had to be the tenth time during my shift that I felt teary where I knew I needed to make a change.

I used a walkie talkie to ask Jordan, a team leader I'd been mentoring, for his location. I'd given him his tasks for the night, changing out a couple of endcaps that had low inventory before the weekend, but I wanted his job. That kind of monotony would help me keep the things at bay I was trying very hard to ignore.

I found him in front of some endcaps in storage, staring at them critically. Jordan was nineteen, just about to start his sophomore year of college, and he was leaning towards business management as a major. I hadn't expected to be given someone to mentor so soon after joining Target myself, but Yvette told me he'd asked specifically for me. The confidence that had given me gave me a huge boost in how I viewed myself at work. I knew I was doing well—my managers told me that frequently—but understanding that the people I managed also felt that I was doing a great job was much more gratifying to me.

"What's up?" he asked, digging through the pile of salesplans I'd given him to work on.

"You're up tonight," I said.

"What do you mean?" he asked, looking from the papers to me in surprise. I'd given him a lot of the basics on what I felt made a good leader, but he hadn't ever taken the reins for longer than to give me time to scarf down a meal.

"Lead," I said, pulling the papers from his hands. "Let me know if you need me for my keys, but otherwise you're ready for this."

"Tonight?" he asked, trying to cover his uncertainty with surprise, but I could see it. It was exactly how I felt when I was given leadership of the store for the first time.

"Yes," I said. "I'm here. If anything goes awry, it's my fault. But it won't." I plucked my walkie from my belt and spoke into it before he could argue any further. "Team," I said into it. "As of this moment, Jordan is going to be your acting LOD. Anything you need, ask him before you ask me. And obviously haze him appropriately."

The chatter back on the walkie was teasing, but supportive. "Go. Check on people. Let me know how trash and cardboard look. Let me know when you want to do huddle," I said of our evening team touch base. "I'll be here. With these hangers," I said, glancing at the cart he had parked in the adjacent aisle.

He was caught off guard, but he was pleased. He'd wanted a moment to show what he was capable of and he finally had it. I was happy to give it, but as soon as he was out of sight, I drew in a shaky breath. I had an excellent mask, but it was so much harder to maintain around people I cared about. That was the part of having a career in retail I hadn't banked on. I knew my mom cared about her team, but I had to come first for so long that I never got to see it in action. I cared about the people I worked with so easily that it was jarring compared to how long it took me to figure out how to care about myself.

It was the right decision for a multitude of reasons to put Jordan in charge, but selfishly I knew it kept me afloat. I wasn't swimming anymore—I knew that my thoughts could easily go to a dark place, that it would be like flipping a switch and, at least temporarily, the despair would swallow me.

Gwen's diagnosis had been much more serious than mine and my mom's, but I'd watched her go through exactly what I did, chemo and surgery, and not come out of it, and it was exactly what kept running through my mind. Not the fear of it happening to me, something that I revisited countless times when I got sick for the second time, but the horrible gut punch of losing a friend. My brain kept trying to imagine what would happen to me if I lost my mom too, and it was dragging me down in a way that I had to force myself out of.

Throughout the night, I set all five of the endcaps I'd tasked Jordan with. I hardly had to check in with him, though I did stop by each of my team members to get a gauge on how he'd done. Everyone loved Jordan—he radiated energy, but he was an introvert, so he was the perfect leader to demonstrate what it was like to be your true self at work. Pride swelled within me again and I held onto it like a life preserver.

It was near close when he approached me hesitantly as I was throwing garbage into the compactor. It was the least sure of himself he'd seemed all night.

"Can I get your help with something?" he asked.

"Depends on what it is," I told him, meaning it. He'd done so well that I wanted his momentum to continue.

"Kelly told me there're some people being a little disruptive at Starbucks," he said. "Can I see how you handle that?"

I held his gaze for a minute. It was what had initially made Yvette the most nervous too, but I was good it at. I understood why correcting someone else's behavior could be unnerving, but for me it was the same way I set expectations with my team. There were already a clear set of expectations for how to act in public. I had no problem holding people accountable to those.

"Sure," I said. "Let's go."

I shared the feedback with him that I'd gathered from the team on our way up front. He was quietly pleased, but he was thrumming with nervous energy as we approached Starbucks.

It'd been closed for a while, but there was a loud group who had pushed a couple small tables together, laughing and rowdy, but otherwise fine.

It was a group I knew how to approach. "Come on, guys," I said from the entrance of Starbucks. "We're not a—"

They weren't going to learn what we weren't, not when my words were caught in my throat. There were five of them, three wearing yellow.

Brody rose to his feet, the cute blonde from the first night at the fair nearly losing her footing as she tumbled out of his lap.

"Jesus, Wash," she grumbled, but he didn't acknowledge her at all.

"Annie?" Brody said in disbelief. The other three roared with laughter at something unrelated and he turned to them in irritation. "Guys, lower the volume." His jaw was sharp and distracting and I had nothing, no words, to handle the situation.

Jordan's elbow was in my side, but it didn't help. I was tongue-tied, the emotions I had been trying so hard to manage way too close to the surface. Had I found Brody twenty-four hours earlier, I imagined my response would have been different, but looking at him in front of me made me think of so many things I wasn't able to handle.

"Keep the volume manageable," Jordan spoke, possessing all of the authority I knew I usually had, "and you're fine," he said. It was exactly how I would have handled the situation and the realization of that was what brought me back to the real world.

"Nice," I said under my breath. I didn't know what to say or do with Brody standing in front of me, staring at me in surprise. I knew what I wanted to do—I wanted to stare. He was even more stunning under the fluorescent lights than he had been in the dim light of sunset, his cheekbones as sharp as his jaw, his face a mastery of symmetry.

But it was awkward, impossible for the people around us not to feel it too, so I turned on my heel and walked away, feeling like I had no other option.

"Hell no," I heard from behind me. It was the guy that had been there the first night of the fair, the one that had dragged Brody away. "After all the talking you've done, you're not letting her walk away." He said to Brody. I felt like I might throw up.

Half a beat of silence passed before Brody spoke. "Annie, wait up," he said.

My heartbeat skyrocketed. Jordan had turned with me and he glanced at me . *Was I okay?* I could read it in his eyes. I had no idea what the answer to that question was, but I nodded anyway. I was fine with Brody. I could handle it. I said it like a mantra before I spoke to Jordan.

"Check in with the rest of the team. Get a feel for when we'll be ready to go. I'm gonna clean up my mess," I told him. He stayed with me for a brief moment, the action entirely to ensure Brody knew I had people on my side.

It took after Jordan disappeared around a corner for Brody to speak. "You work here," he said, realizing how lame he sounded so he spoke again quickly. "What do you do?"

"I run food," I told him.

"Like mother like daughter then," he said, and I froze. I wasn't ready to talk about her, to think about her, but his words were extremely apt, and I could feel the despair again.

"Yeah," I forced myself to say something. "I have to clean up. If you want to talk, come with me."

He nodded and fell into step with me, easily matching my quick stride with his long legs. I was grateful for the pile of boxes waiting for me to break down, needing to do something with my hands.

He seemed at a loss for words, but eventually landed on what was the most obvious thing he could say. "Twice in like ten days," he said. "After nothing for ten years. Weird, right?"

I shrugged. "Right now, I'm going more with awkward." It was meant to be a joke, but my tone was wrong. I shook my head. "How do you still frazzle me?" I said without thinking.

He chuckled and his body language relaxed. It was what he needed to hear. "I thought that was just happening to me," he admitted.

"What do you mean?" I asked him. "Your friend back there. What have you been talking about?"

He chuckled again, rubbing the back of his neck nervously. His tattoos were still impossible to make out with the space between us, but they twisted up his forearm to his bicep, something I hadn't noticed before. "I see you're still as point blank as ever."

"I try to be," I admitted, turning my attention to my task. "A lot's happened in ten years. And you didn't answer my question."

"I've been thinking about you," he said, watching as I broke down boxes. My hands were shaking, my heart hammering, and I'd been kidding myself if I thought I was looking for anything other than a true connection with him. "Pretty much all week. I thought I was playing it cool enough. Guess not."

I took a deep breath. My focus was waning and not in a good way. "Brody," I said, but he spoke before I could.

"God, that's strange to hear. Besides my mom, no one calls me that anymore."

"Wash," I realized, remembering what the blonde had called him. It didn't feel right, not for me. Not that it mattered.

"I have to finish up here," I told him. "It's my store for the night. There are things—"

"What if I wait for you?" he offered. "Second time in ten days, Annie. Let's have the conversation the universe wants us to have."

"It could be a while," I said. I had become pretty excellent at determining when we'd be able to leave by how much work we had left to do before close, but

I'd been intentionally leaving that in Jordan's hands, so I didn't know for sure.

"We've waited ten years. What's another hour?" He smiled and the butterflies in my stomach were fluttering so wildly I felt sick. "I'll be outside. It's a beautiful night."

"Okay," I said, proud of how even my voice was. "Then I'll see you in an hour or so."

I let out a shaky breath, shameless while watching him walk away. His black jeans were snug and I watched until he was gone.

"You are not good enough at hiding," I said to Jordan, who was on the back end of the aisle I was standing in front of. His walkie had squealed at one point during my conversation, so I'd known it wasn't private.

He stepped into the aisle, holding his hands up in surrender. "It's only like twenty percent curiosity, Annie," he insisted. "The rest was concern."

"Which I why I didn't call you out on it before," I told him. "For the record, you did great quieting them. That's what I would have said if I'd had the power of speech at that point."

He burst out laughing. "Who's the guy?"

"Someone I knew a long time ago," I said. "Didn't expect to see him. Don't worry about it. You have a closing email to write. I've got doors to lock and cardboard to get rid of. How long until we're out of here?"

"Probably fifty minutes," he said. "Team's working fast, may be sooner."

"Great," I said. "Get going. I'll meet you up front after I'm done with this," I gestured to the tub full of cardboard.

He saluted me and I headed towards the backroom, my head spinning. Brody was outside. He was waiting for me. And I had no idea what I wanted to say to him. It was the best distraction from my mom that I could have asked for. It brought up a lot of emotions, but my emotions related to Brody were not the same as the fear I had about losing my mom.

I tossed the cardboard into the baler and did my best to clear my mind of all of it. Being level-headed felt like a smart thing, but I'd have to work for it.

I was intercepted by Yvette halfway towards the doors. "I locked them," she said in a rush.

"What are you even doing here? Don't you work at ten tomorrow?" I asked in surprise.

"Giving them half a night," she shrugged. "You know I like it. Do you know who's outside, Annie?"

I nodded slowly and Yvette squealed. "You found him? Is that why you've been MIA all day? And last night, you minx."

I shook my head. Her excited expression was shifting to something else and I realized my mask was not as firmly in place as I wanted. "What's going on?" She asked, then she barreled forward. "And for what it's worth, that tell I mentioned—when you're about to lie—you're doing it right now."

"He showed up here," I said. It wasn't a lie. It was entirely true. "We're going to talk."

"That's not what's bothering you," she said gently. "Annie, I'm not going to push you. But you've come a long way, and all I want to do is help you, you know that."

I pushed on the corners of my eyes, abruptly teary. It took me a moment to even understand why Yvette had undone me so quickly. She knew so much more than anyone else, so she knew how to read me, but more than that, I liked talking to her. Sharing with her had been cathartic, but giving into that, sharing the details of my mom's diagnosis, it would start the spiral I was desperately avoiding.

"I can't talk about it and still be able to talk to him," I told her.

"Okay," she said instantly, reaching for my hands and squeezing them.

"I'll call you tomorrow, okay?" I said.

"I'll come over," she shook her head. "After work. I'll bring wine and we can binge watch old episodes of *Scandal* and you can tell me what's going on, okay?"

I nodded, pushing hard against my eyes again. I left her for the front of the store, checking in on Jordan briefly, but I bypassed him for my office. I needed a moment alone, a couple seconds where no one was watching me, or I was going to lose it.

I shut the door to my office once I was inside it. It was tiny, no bigger than a small closet, and I shared it with the other food leader, but we intentionally worked opposite shifts, so we were never in each other's way. I gripped the back of my chair, my fingernails piercing the fabric, and I allowed myself sixty seconds to wallow. I held back my tears, knowing I'd be a mess if I cried, both physically and mentally, but a sob escaped before I could stop it. I was toeing a dangerous line; it was going to be easy to push me over it.

I grabbed my phone out of my purse, hoping my mom had texted. I needed reassurance that she was okay, and she didn't disappoint. I had one message, a picture of her fanning herself with several twenty dollar bills, with a caption saying *maybe my luck is changing. Love you.*

I smiled. *Dinner's on you when you get back. <3*

My hands stopped shaking, her message stabilizing me. I took a deep breath and rejoined the rest of the Target world, surprised to find the team already clocking out.

"Don't look at me," Jordan said the moment I did look at him. "Evie said they can handle cleaning up the fitting room; it's all that's left. I don't argue with her."

I shook my head. Yvette was trying to make my life easier by trying to get me to Brody sooner. I wasn't sure if that was actually going to make my life easier or a hell of a lot harder, but I was open to finding out. "Okay, did you send the email?" I asked and he nodded. "Punch out. Jordan, you were fantastic tonight. Thank you. Consider all your shifts with me LOD shifts if you want it."

"I think I do," he grinned. "But let's see how my classes go." His grin softened. "Whatever's on your mind, I hope it gets better, Annie. I'll see you soon."

"Thanks," I said, oddly touched. I knew I hadn't been myself, but I hadn't expected him to comment on it or to understand that I was struggling. "Have a good night."

I let the team head out, watching them from the door until they all drove away. I didn't miss Jordan approach the bench on the east side of the property. I knew Brody had to be over there; Jordan paused for less than a minute before he got into his car and left.

"What are you still doing here?" Yvette asked from behind me.

"Mildly panicking," I replied instantaneously and she snickered. "Do you ever feel like your expectations are too high?"

She shook her head. "I think that's one of the major differences between the two of us, my dear Annabel. I don't. I think we should expect a lot of people. It tends to make them rise to the challenge," her gaze was pointed as I considered that. It worked for me to be sure—she'd been delicate, but she had expected me to engage and be present so I was. I couldn't disagree with her methods.

"Go talk to him," she said. "What do you have to lose?"

"Right now—too much," I admitted, but continued before she could address it and before my nausea could return. "But nothing he's responsible for. You're right. But is it vain that I wish I wasn't wearing this?"

She laughed. "Uh, no. That man is like a sculptured god. How did you leave that out?!"

"It was dark!" I exclaimed, letting her lead me back to her office.

"I actually have the shorts you lent me," she said. "And I'm sure you have a tank top on under that shirt."

"It is not warm enough for that," I laughed. "And I don't think I want to look like I'm trying so hard. Why bother?"

"Valid," she said. "Undo your braid."

"Why?" I could still feel my mom's fingers in my hair. Undoing it felt like I would be undoing that.

"It's getting messy," she said. "And he knew you when you were sick, honey. Let him see you when you're not."

I nodded slowly. She was right about that. I lived in scarves and headwraps during the couple of months he'd known me a decade ago. Emotionally I didn't feel like I was at one hundred percent—I felt like I'd just found ninety percent only days before—but physically I was the healthiest I'd ever been, excluding all of the fair food I'd eaten over the past ten days. I undid the braid, weaving my fingers through it, gripping it near the base of my neck for a moment like I was gripping my mom's hand, before I shook out the rest.

Yvette fixed my part for me, her hand dropping on my shoulder. "Annie, this doesn't have to be anything other than a conversation between two people who haven't seen each other in a decade. You get to make it what you want it to be."

"Thank you," I told her. "And thank you for being here, Evie. I love you, you know."

She grinned. "I love you, too. Tomorrow. We're hashing out what's bothering you, don't forget."

"I'm actually looking forward to the company," I assured her. I squeezed her hand once, gathered the courage I had, and I headed outside.

DAY TEN

I didn't realize it was past midnight until I walked by our closed cash register bank, the first one I saw flashing a time of two minutes past twelve. It felt mildly ridiculous, meeting a guy I knew ten years ago in a parking lot, but my pace didn't slow as I exited the building, locking the door behind me.

Brody stood as I approached. He'd been playing on his phone, but as soon as he caught me in his periphery, he stuffed it in his pocket and stood, waiting for me.

The awkwardness was back, but we were both aware of it, and that made it easier to manage. "You didn't think I'd show," I teased.

"I did think it was possible you'd never leave the building," he admitted, a small smile on his face.

"I have a question," I said. "I have a million questions. But one that I want you to answer right now."

"Okay," he said hesitantly.

"What goddamn booth do you work for?" I asked, gesturing at his yellow shirt.

He laughed. "Flowering Onion," he said.

"Are you serious?!" I squeaked in surprise. I'd been there probably a half dozen times while volunteering with MINMIC, but I hadn't seen him or the other two I recognized. "That's like my favorite one."

"I remember that," he admitted and I looked at him in surprise. "Annie, what did we not talk about? There are so many situations—even now—when I think, I know exactly what you would say or do or how you would act, and maybe it's not even true anymore, but it was ten years ago."

"I looked for you," I admitted and it was his turn to be surprised. I was somewhat surprised myself that I wasn't embarrassed to share it. "Thursday. More than that, really. I've been doing some volunteering inside the fairgrounds, so basically anytime someone walked by in yellow, I looked up." I shrugged and laughed. "I was starting to think I'd imagined you."

He was quiet for a long moment, but his body language was still open. "I saw you again," he said slowly. I took an unconscious step back. If he'd had the opportunity to approach me again and didn't, we were on two very different pages regarding what we were hoping to find.

"You were with some fit soccer player so I left you alone," he added after another long pause.

I barked out a laugh. "Juan," I shook my head. "Jesus. This is all too much."

How did I tell him what seemed so plain to me now? I'd been trying to get him out of my head and Juan was a welcome distraction. It had been a decade and Brody had worked his way well beneath my skin. I glanced up at the CCTV cameras and wrapped my arms around myself. "Can we go for a walk?" I asked, knowing Yvette well enough to know she'd be dissecting our body language in the assets protection office.

Brody nodded. I waved at the camera then and he laughed, falling into step beside me. I tossed my purse in my car and we headed east.

"You got people here that care about you," he acknowledged.

I nodded. "As much as I tried to get them not to."

"Sounds familiar," he teased, and it didn't hurt, thinking of before. I felt a sort of nostalgia, but my emotions felt somewhat muted. I had my fear in a vice grip. It wasn't going to come out if I could help it. "That kid you were working with had words for me."

"I saw that," I cringed. "What embarrassing thing did he say?"

"Nothing like that," he admitted. "He called you a warrior. Said not to fuck with you." I snorted. "I told him you'd always been a warrior and I never had the ability to change that."

I glanced over at him, feeling pride and something else stirring beneath the surface. He sounded far away and I knew he was thinking of Gwen. "I miss her," I said. "I think about her constantly. I see her everywhere."

"Me too," he admitted. "Even more since I saw you again."

"Tell me about you, Brods," I said, trying to coax him out the past. "Because Googling you doesn't work."

He laughed. "No, probably not. What'd you find out?"

"You got good at football," I said, then shrugged. "Everything I learned came from Juan. He gave me a neat summary."

Brody came to a stop at that. "The soccer player? I feel like that needs explanation. He seemed into you."

I shook my head. I didn't know what could have happened between me and Juan, but that would have been a world where Yvette didn't exist, and that wasn't a world I wanted to be in. I didn't know how to explain any of it—it was all too personal for the situation we were in. "He told me you're an accountant," I said. "Went to school in North Dakota for economics and accounting. Not what I would have guessed."

We came to a stop at a red light on Hamline, intending to go south. He looked down at me, his expression impossible to read, but I held his gaze. "I don't think I knew what I wanted to do until I had to pick something," he admitted. "Football made it so I didn't have to. I landed on something I thought would be boring and it's not." He shrugged. "And you end up doing exactly what your mom does. Not what I would have thought either."

I nodded, tearing my eyes away. The fear was there again. Being with Brody, thinking about Gwen—my emotions may have felt muted, but it was still terrifying to remember how I'd felt about losing Gwen and then think about losing my mother as well. The light changed and I nudged him forward, grateful that I could hide my expression in the dark.

"Why is this so difficult?" he asked, his tone light. "We used to be able to talk about anything."

"Ten years is a long time," I pointed out. "I don't know about you, but life got harder after Gwen died, not easier. It didn't get easier for years."

He nodded. "Are you happy now, Annie?"

"I don't know," I admitted. "I don't think I've fully figured out how to be. Are you?"

"I am," he said. "Losing Gwen defined my life for so long; letting that go was how I healed. Took a while to figure it out, but once I did… I'm happy now."

"Good job, you spend twelve days deep frying onions with a pretty blonde—life is good?"

"Are you fishing for info, Annie Banannie?" I could hear the grin in his voice.

"I don't think I need it. She was in your lap," I reminded him, my tone much more chill than I felt. I was fishing for information because I did want to know if he was single, and it shouldn't matter. I wasn't sure why it did matter, but I desperately wanted him to tell me.

"I did kiss you ten days ago."

"I remember," I said, ignoring the thunk in my chest.

"I don't kiss more than one person at a time," he said, and I ignored my relief. "Chelsey's a friend."

"She wants to be more." I wanted to slap my hand over my mouth. I hadn't intended to say that at all.

"Want to tell me about Juan?"

"Not at all," I admitted, glancing around. I hadn't been paying much attention to where I was walking, not even realizing that I was the one leading us, until I noticed how close we were to home.

"You were looking for me Thursday," he said. "Why?"

"I don't know," I said, and it was a lie. I did know. The way my heart was beating, I knew exactly what I had been lying to myself about. We'd had fifteen minutes after a decade of nothing and all I wanted was more. It felt like I'd been holding my breath for years and finally came up for air only to be submerged again, and I hadn't fully realized that until I had him in front of me again. I felt calm. I felt a sense of peace I hadn't had since before Gwen died. I hadn't known how much I wanted it until I had it, and there was a part of me that wasn't sure I deserved it.

"I think that's bullshit," he said softly.

"Our conversation was cut short," I replied. "I wanted to see where it could have gone. You and Gwen were the first people I felt like I didn't have to pretend with—it's exhausting. It's still exhausting."

We stopped at a red light on Garden Avenue— we were only a street away from Larpenteur, a block from my apartment. He stopped close enough to me that I bumped into him. I took a half-step back, closing my eyes. "You're not pretending now? You're not wearing that mask now?" he asked, point-blank.

"Of course I am," I bit back, and the wall I had built up against my emotions broke. "I don't know you anymore. You don't know me. The last time I was open with you, you left. I know she died. I know that's the worst thing anyone would have to go through. I know it because I had to go through it too—but I had to do it alone. We were just kids— god, how does anyone survive what we went through?" I shook my head, turning away from him, abruptly ashamed. "I'm sorry," I told him. "We were just kids."

"It's on me," he said. "You're right about that. Annie—look at me."

I shook my head, feeling too unstable for the conversation we were having. He tapped me on the jaw, an action he'd done dozens of times when we were kids and I wasn't giving him the attention he wanted, and it broke me. I wrapped my fingers around his and turned to him, taking a shaky breath. "When I think about you, it always comes back to this," he said. The light had changed, but I was rooted to the spot, and he made no move to continue our journey. "I should have come back for you. You couldn't come for me. You were sick too—what were you going to do? We were both kids, but it was a conscious choice on my part to stay away from you. I'm sorry. God, I'm sorry."

I could feel the tears in the corners of my eyes and I stepped away from him, closing my eyes tight. He sunk a tentative hand into my hair, wrapping curls around his fingers, and I drew on his strength. It had always been something he'd been able to give me— the idea that I was perfect as-is. I hadn't found a way to imitate that feeling, but it was back so clearly it was as if it had never left.

He wrapped his arms around me in a hug and I pressed my cheek against his chest, watching the light change to red again. He was firm and warm and smelled like onions and I could have stood like that forever. "Can we have this conversation?" he asked. His body thrummed as he spoke. "Can we work through the guilt and the blame and see where we come out?"

I nodded, dropping my arms from him. "I live like two blocks away. Come on."

Neither of us spoke again, but he walked close beside me, and when our hands brushed, he captured mine. My body felt electric, the innocence of hand-holding causing the same physical reaction it had when I was twelve and he hooked his pinky around mine for the first time.

We were inside my apartment before we spoke again. His eyes immediately went to my bed, and his grin was slow and pleased, but not for the reason anyone else would think. My bed was pushed up against the wall that the window was on—if I tilted my head back, I could see the stars.

I had a recliner and a desk chair, but it didn't matter. We both kicked our shoes off and laid on our backs, looking up out the window. Out a clear sense of vanity, I was happy my mom had busied herself with making my bed while I'd showered because it wasn't something I did often.

He reclaimed my hand again, his grip loose, his thumb making lazy patterns against the inside of my wrist. "I still sleep like this too," he admitted.

"I made my mom move my bed," I said. "When I went home after surgery. I annoyed every college roommate I had. It made me feel in control of something."

"Tell me about you, Annie," he said. "What were you like in college? What do you do for fun? Pretend we don't have all of this shit in the past and maybe we can figure out how to navigate it."

I shrugged. It was a lot easier to start with college, to start with the beginning of my healing then with how hard my teenage years had been. And as I told him about how hard school was for me, how lonely I was, even though they weren't easy things to say, I found that I wanted to tell him.

He was contemplative when I finished telling him about Paula and Yvette and work. His thumb wove a nearly constant pattern against my skin, but it would stop when he was digesting something I'd said, and he'd stopped at a few things that made my heart pound. I'd said nearly nothing about my mom, glossing over it when he'd asked about her. It was difficult to refocus after that.

I rolled onto my side, propping myself up on my elbow. I released his hand, but I tugged on his arm, finally able to take in all of the tattoos in his sleeve. I couldn't stop myself from touching them, picking out Gwen's initials within an extremely detailed pattern on his forearm. There were letters and numbers, nothing I could make any sense of, but it looked like a timeline or something. I was intrigued. "Tell me about these," I said softly.

"I have one more question," he said softly. "And then I will."

"Shoot," I said.

"Your soccer player. What is that?"

I chuckled and shook my head. "He's in love with Evie. They just reconnected. There's nothing going on there."

He turned onto his side too, his palm resting against my cheek, and my eyes fluttered closed. "I'm going to answer every question you have," he said. "But right now I'm going to kiss you, if that's something you—"

I didn't wait for him to finish his question, pushing my lips against his. It was nothing like the kisses of our teens, which were hesitant and explorative, because we had years and experience between us, and all I wanted was to feel him under my hands.

When we finally broke apart, we were gasping. For as long as it had taken us to explore the skin beneath our shirts before, both of our hands were already there. My hands pressed against his lower back, holding him tightly against me.

He kissed my forehead. "What does this feel like to you? Is this just me?" He sounded half-drunk, so I knew what he meant.

I brought one hand up to his face, enjoying the sandpaper feeling of his beard against it. "It's not just you. It's not. I felt like—I saw you again for fifteen minutes and I couldn't get you out of my head."

"I haven't been able to either," he admitted. "And then I saw you with Juan and I think I understood it— or there was no reason to pretend that I wasn't jealous."

"You could have found me," I said. "I'm a typical twenty-two year old woman at least in terms of social media. You could have found me."

"I saw you with him, Annie," he reminded me. "I didn't think you wanted to be found."

"I was trying to reset," I said, pressing my lips to his jaw. "I felt like a lunatic," I said against his neck. "It was all self-preservation."

"Because I left you before."

"Yes," I said.

"I'm sorry, Annie," he said, catching my chin with his fingers and he kissed me hard on the mouth.

"You're supposed to be telling me about your tattoos," I said when we separated.

"I like how they feel," he said, tugging me against him. "Which isn't the answer I give anyone else. But eighteen-year-old, masochist me really enjoyed the pain. So I kept going back. The pattern doesn't mean anything to me—it was time-consuming and painful and my adrenaline was sky high when it was done. I loved it."

"I see Gwen's initials," I traced my fingers over them. "So it's not entirely meaningless. Which one was your first?"

"It's on my chest," he said, rolling onto his back to pull his onion-scented tee shirt over his head. Below his collarbone, from the center of his chest to near his right armpit, he had a Shakespearian phrase permanently inked on his body. *Though she is but little, she is fierce!*

I traced it with my fingertips, hard muscle against my skin, feeling teary again. "She would have thought this was the cheesiest thing in the world," I said despite myself and he burst out laughing.

"She really would have," he agreed. "But she wasn't the only one on my mind when I got it." His fingers wove their way into my hair again. "Is that crazy?"

"Maybe a little," I said and he laughed. I pressed my lips to the tattoo, my heart beating rapidly.

"I didn't really think it through," he admitted. "Doesn't exactly score me any points when I have a tattoo about another woman on my chest. Bit of a mood-killer whether I bother to explain it or not." I laughed, resting my cheek against his chest. I could see that it would be awkward. Not explaining it would likely be the better option, better than talking about his dead sister and first girlfriend.

"So you went to college on a football scholarship. When did you get in interested in football?"

"After Gwen died. When someone told me I could hit people and not get in trouble for it," he said. "I had a lot of anger. They should have put me on an

D-line or something with as nasty as I was, but it turned out I'm pretty good at catching a football, so…"

"Do you still play?"

He shook his head. "No. No interest once I figured out how to manage that anger. I play basketball with some friends to stay in shape and work through any aggression."

"And you count other people's money," I said teasingly, still not understanding how he'd found a career so far off what from he'd been interested in as a teen.

He smiled, his hand resting against my hip. "I know, it's weird. My parents thought I was bluffing when I chose it. I was hard for them to deal with— you know? I think they thought I'd drop out just to spite them, but I wasn't ever mad at them. It was the universe. I stopped going to church and it hit them hard, but I couldn't believe in a religion that would strip Gwen from us. I still haven't figured that piece out."

I nodded. My mom had never been religious, so I didn't grow up religiously, but when I thought about it on my own, I knew I'd never get there. I'd been through too much to trust in an omnipotent being without having a significant amount of disdain for it. I hadn't believed in anything bigger than myself until the fair kept throwing people at each other, throwing the best and worst parts of my past in my face, and I'd come out stronger.

"How'd you manage that anger, Brody?" I asked. I expected his answer was different than mine in terms of the way he spoke about it. I felt slightly hesitant as I waited for his response.

"It's going to sound New Age and hippie," he shook his head. He was hesitant, too. I could hear it in his tone. He didn't want to be dismissed. "But I tried everything. I tried therapy and anti-everythings, and the only thing that made any difference for me is meditation. And yoga. It's been a journey, but I figured it out. I really am happier than I think I've been since she died." He turned to me, his fingers on my hip bone. "What about you, Annie? How'd you manage?"

"I didn't," I answered. "I'm only now figuring it out. Therapy, and antidepressants," I admitted. "But I don't think I'm ready to talk about that part of my life yet." Too much of it was tied to my mom, but bringing up nearly dying, and then wanting to die, was heavy and painful. I paused for a moment, trying to determine if I wanted to say what I was thinking, but I decided I didn't have much to lose if I did. "I worry about slipping back. It was dark. I was…" I trailed off. "I'm not ready."

He kissed my hair. "I'm good with that, Annie. You said it before. Ten years is a long time. We don't need to hash it all out tonight."

My heartbeat slowed gratefully and I yawned. I hadn't expected him to be pushy, but it was still a load off my shoulders. "Where do you live?" I asked him. His family had been in the south metro, but I assumed he had his own place at twenty-four.

"Like ten minutes from here," he laughed. "I bought a house in the Como neighborhood last year." I jolted in surprise and he squeezed me and laughed again. "All of my friends have one bedrooms in the North Loop and I live in a neighborhood full of retirees. I love it."

It wasn't why I was surprised. It was where he'd wanted to live when we were kids. He was right; we did talk about everything back then. He'd talked about the houses and the parks and the zoo. I hadn't been there. I hadn't spent much time in the metro area until I got sick, but I went in college. I explored the neighborhood, pretending that he wasn't the reason why. I shook my head. I'd thought of him frequently, but it amazed me that I hid so much about what that meant even from myself.

"Brody?" I said, the adrenaline of reconnecting with him petering out. It was late and I was tired.

"Hmm?"

"Put your number in my phone. Right now. I'm not losing you again," I said, handing him the device from my back pocket.

He took it, entering in his info and texting himself from my phone. "Annie?"

"Yeah?"

"You need to be upfront with me right now. Do you want me to go?" He asked, his voice sounding as sleepy as mine felt.

"I want you to stay," I said. "Just like this."

"I could do this forever."

"Don't over-promise," I shot back and he laughed.

"Never," he assured me. He kissed my hair again and I fell asleep wrapped up in him, my mind blank.

• • •

I gasped awake in the early morning hours. My mind had been empty when I'd fallen asleep, but just like when I was sick, my dreams were plagued by worst-case scenarios.

Emotionally, Friday had been one of the most intense days of my life. Finding Brody again and admitting to all of the things I'd been avoiding was big enough, but learning my mom was sick with cancer, the same thing that had upended our lives before, was what wove through my dreams.

The sun was on its way up, but my bed was empty. It took me a moment to even remember that Brody had stayed the night, my breathing still so uneven from the dream. So frequently my dreams were about the dead—people I cared about who were already dead or who weren't, but they always asked why they had to die when I had wanted to so badly. It was something I still couldn't manage all of the time. I didn't want to die anymore, but my subconscious wanted to remind me often that I had a lot of shame about it.

"Annie?" Brody asked quietly. It took me a moment to find him in the dark. He was sitting cross-legged on the floor, his yellow shirt back on, and I could tell by his body language that he had been meditating.

I sat up and bolted for the bathroom, the nausea I'd pushed down the day before coming back in full force. My brain had shown me my mother in various states of decomposition throughout the night, and flashing through them made it impossible to settle my stomach.

Brody hovered in the doorway. It wasn't the first time he'd watched me heave. Chemo had taken a toll on me and he'd patiently sat with me while I spent hours sick.

He looked mildly alarmed when I caught his reflection in the mirror, but he rested a hand on my back gently. "Déjà vu," he said softly. "You okay?"

I shrugged, taking a deep breath. I stepped away from the toilet and rinsed my mouth with water, closing my eyes tightly. I could still see her, still hear the questions that had eaten at me for so long, and I knew I wasn't okay. I wasn't even close.

"Do you want me to show you what I do?" he asked me.

I shook my head. I didn't buy it enough, didn't believe that it would help, so I knew I'd never commit enough to it in the moment for it to actually work.

"Can I have a minute?" I asked. "I'll get it together," I said.

I was looking at him in the mirror, not turning to face him, and his expression was impossible to discern. "By burying it?" he asked. His tone was gentle. He was trying to help, but I viscerally did not want it.

"Brody," I said. "Just give me a minute."

"Okay," he squeezed my shoulder and stepped out and I waited until the door closed behind him before I took a gasping breath. I was going to need more than a minute. I was usually better at getting past the horrors in my dreams, but so much had come out in the last twenty-four hours that I felt like I had nearly none of the control I usually possessed.

I brushed my teeth while I thought through nearly all of the coping mechanisms I'd used in the past. Some were Matt approved, most were not, and ultimately I landed on doing exactly what Brody thought I'd do—I buried it.

It was ineffective and wouldn't last long. I wanted to talk to my mom, but I would worry her if I called. I decided to text her, taking a deep breath before I rejoined Brody on the other side of the door.

I picked up my phone and shot her a text. It was early, but we never operated on a normal schedule, so that on its own wouldn't be enough to concern her.

The awkwardness was settling in again. It had been easy to reconnect once we'd gotten past it, but I had no idea what that meant for the future. I didn't know what it meant for the moment we were in. "I don't know what you want me to do," Brody broke the silence. His tone was still gentle, but he seemed on edge.

"I'm making things harder for you," I realized. He was trying to maintain his balance, but instability was impacting him. "Brody, I'm sorry."

He shook his head. "It's not that. I want to help you."

"I'm not ready to let you," I admitted.

"Why?" he asked. "There's only one reason I can think of, and I only know it because I remember it myself."

"Brody," I began warningly, but he shook his head again.

"You think you don't deserve it. Why?" he continued. My heart thumped in my chest. It was the truth, what was at the core of most of my unresolved issues. I felt undeserving of the good things I had because of how close I'd come to cutting them all off.

It was one of the things I'd never addressed in therapy, something I hadn't felt until I realized how grateful I was to still be alive. In terms of my road to recovery, it was a relatively new roadblock, and one I'd had managed before my mom shared her news. I was poisonous. Wanting to die and hating to live made everyone else around me pay. It was impossible to shed the blame once it got a foothold, and it had an epic one.

I shook my head at him. He wasn't capable of helping me. That was on me.

"Annie," he said. "I know some breathing exercises that saved me and—"

I held up a hand. "I can't do this. Let it go."

"I remember what this felt like," he said. "I would have given anything for someone to step in."

"That's bullshit," I said, and I felt a piece inside me snap. He took a step back in surprise. He had been through a lot, but my suffering was mine. The only claim he had to it was that his departure had made it worse. "If you had a clue what I was feeling, you'd know I mean it when I say I don't want help. I've got it."

His gaze was intense. "That's the thing, Annie. You don't."

It was my turn to be surprised. He was right, but besides Matt, no one ever called me out on that. "Just go," I said. "I'm not a project. You don't owe me anything."

"I owe you everything," he said vehemently. "You are the reason I made it through losing her."

My tears were sudden and hot and I was mortified. I brushed them off my cheeks. "You left me behind! I'm glad I made your life so fucking easy while I had to do it all alone."

He didn't wince at my words so I knew he'd thought worse. "Annie, you came out the other side of all of that."

"Yeah, and I'm in great goddamn shape," I wiped my cheeks, and the despair I'd been fighting so hard finally broke through. "You made the right choice ten years ago. Get on with your life."

"That's what I'm trying to do," he said softly. "And for ten years, I've missed you and thought about you and had every possible 'what-if' run through my head. I want the chance to explore it. Tell me you don't feel that way too, like you can finally breathe right. Like you're not missing a part of you."

I shook my head fervently. "I'm missing several parts."

"Annie, come on," he reached for me but I dodged him, and the way I could so easily still read that I'd hurt his feelings made me cry again.

"You think you ran through all the what-ifs? I guarantee you didn't get anywhere near reality," I spat. I wanted to hurt him. I didn't deserve him. "Gwen died. You left! And all I had was my terrified and lonely mother." I bit down on my lip. "I couldn't say anything about how terrified and lonely I was too because she would have taken that on like she was the one that did it to me, but she wasn't. She's only ever made decisions to make my world better, at the expense of herself." I bit my lip again, my eyes filling with the same terrified tears that had spilled over the day before.

He looked as heartbroken as I felt, which only made me feel worse. "Annie—"

"No," I said, my heart aching. "No. While you made the decision to stay intentionally away from me, I had surgery. I healed. Never emotionally, not completely. I was Annie-with-cancer, tumor-free or not. And then, wouldn't you know, I got sick again. And I got mad. I was alone! So was that one of your what-ifs, Brody? Your sick and lonely first girlfriend that almost died the second time around?" I took in his expression, viciously pleased to watch his eyes widen. "I should have. It would have been easier for everyone if I had."

"Jesus Christ, Annie, that's the least true thing I've ever heard," he said, his voice desperate.

I shook my head. "It gets worse. Do you want to know? I wanted to die. I made a very serious plan, and I was talked out of it because of what it would do to my mom," his gaze broke from mine. I'd done it. I'd said enough to push him away. "So I lived, for her, and I hated her for it. These last several years would have been a lot easier for her if I'd died during surgery. Who knows? Maybe she wouldn't have been run so ragged that she wouldn't now have the same fucking illness that keeps destroying everything worth saving."

His silence was long and powerful, but I didn't move. When he spoke, he sounded broken. "That includes you, Annie," he said softly.

"I'm beyond saving. Take the out," I said, pushing on my eyelids. "Run while you still can."

"I don't—"

"I need you to go," I said quietly. "I can't give you what you're looking for."

"I found what I'm looking for," he said simply. He sounded raw, like I'd ripped him open. My entire body felt numb and I couldn't look at him without wanting to cry. He pressed his lips to my forehead. "I hope I see you around, Annie," he said, and he was gone.

• • •

I spent the better part of the morning in tears. Objectively I knew that I was punishing myself. I took the shame and the grief and the terror about my mom being sick and it became my penance. I felt responsible for all of it, even if the therapy-improved part of my brain knew I wasn't. I'd had a blissful couple of hours of happiness, but my subconscious had destroyed it in seconds, had made me dream of the thing I was most afraid of, and I couldn't handle it.

At noon, when I felt like I was losing even that outside sense of objectivity, I called Matt. "Not coming again?" he said teasingly when he picked up.

"Probably not the best idea," I replied after a beat. Though I thought I was the appropriate amount of self-deprecating, he knew better than that.

"Where are you?" he asked immediately.

"At home," I said. "Snelling and Larpenteur."

"I'll be right there," he said. "You remember some of the mental exercises we used to do?"

"Yeah," I said. "They're not working."

"Start with the physical ones," he said. He sounded like he was moving quickly. "How tense are your shoulders?"

"Tense," I replied. My whole body hurt from the dry-heaving and vomiting. He walked me through releasing the tension a muscle group at a time, and he was at my door before I was done with my abdomen.

"Hey," he said, taking me in. I was a mess, still in my clothes from the day before, with bed head and a splotchy face. He sat me down in my recliner, grabbed my desk chair, and sat directly in front of me, and he offered up his hands.

It was something that worked before. My entire life was spent being manhandled by doctors and nurses, people who were only trying to save my life, but it made casual touch awkward for me. I didn't know what to do with it; my mind would immediately go back to a clinical setting, and I would freeze up, back inside my twelve and sixteen year old mind, a place I hadn't wanted to be then and definitely didn't want to be afterward.

I'd been having a panic attack when we found it the first time. He'd put out his hands, holding them flat, palms up, and I had to try to hold mine just above without touching him. It was bizarre, but it sharpened my mind, it made me focus, and when I finally pushed my hands against his, it was because I wanted to.

It worked again. My heart rate steadied, my breath regulated, and I burst into tears. He returned the pressure, wrapping his hands around mine. "I know you think you're not doing well," he said. "I know you're judging yourself, but I want you to know that you've done an incredible thing. You asked for help when you felt beyond reason. That's a huge accomplishment, Annie." I didn't respond, but if there was one thing he was used to from me, it was my silence. I didn't often know what to say, but I digested slowly, and he left me thoughtful a majority of the time.

"You tell me what you want this to be, okay?" he said, putting the control back in my hands. "What are you fighting?"

I hadn't known when I called him how much I'd want to tell him, but I knew looking at him in his MINMIC shirt and jeans, with the same concerned and proud expression he'd had for me for years, that I was going to tell him everything. It took a while—it wasn't that I lost my focus because I knew exactly what I wanted to say, but how to say it was something I struggled with frequently.

I told him about my mom, about Brody, about that relatively new shame that could swallow me whole, and I'd known him well enough to be able to tell that that was what he locked onto. That shame would be his focus, as long as I'd let him talk about it.

"You didn't forfeit your right to happiness, Annie," he told me. "Do you know that?"

"Sometimes," I said. "I was doing okay until my mom told me she's sick. Now I feel like that's my fault."

"That's the anxiety talking," he reminded me.

"I know," I nodded. I pulled my knees up to my chin. "I always know it. And like I said, I was managing it, but this..." I shook my head. "It was so selfish of me."

"It was not," he said, like I knew he would, like he had dozens of times in the past. "You weren't being spiteful. You've been battling depression for years. Your hormones were beating you down and you tried to find a way out, and in spite of that, you still reached out for help."

"That's not why I called back then," I shook my head. My mind had been made up long before I picked up the phone. I wanted someone to hear me, for me to finally speak the truth.

"I wholeheartedly disagree with you on that," he said. I knew that. It was a conversation we'd had multiple times before and it stuck out because it was one of the only things he hadn't been able to get me to consider his point of view on.

"It's making me feel crazy," I said. "I finally know I want to be here. I feel it with certainty, finally, and I won't allow myself to be happy."

"You're on a journey, Annie," he reminded me. "Depression doesn't disappear. And you know your inner voice is a brutal one. You called her a bitch once," he pointed out. I had in one of our last sessions. "She's like the mean girl you can't ignore, right? That just makes it worse. Will you try something for me?"

"Don't I always?" I replied.

His smile was soft. "There was a time when that was a very strong no." I snorted despite myself. That was also true.

"You need to shut her up," he said. "And we're going to try to do that with evidence. What's she saying to you right now? We don't have to start with the hardest one."

"They're all hard," I muttered. "But okay. I lost all the progress I made."

"What do you think?"

"I agree with her on that one."

"Think about a time before the progress then. Tell me what you would have done then if you felt she was getting too loud."

"I don't know," I admitted. "Gone to bed, probably."

"Is that managing or avoiding?"

"Feels like a little of both."

"It probably is," he granted me that. "So you wouldn't have called me?"

I knew the answer was no, but it wasn't that simple. "You weren't in my life in this fixed point I'm thinking of."

"Fine, you wouldn't have sought out help? You would have managed on your own?"

"Yes," I allowed. "I would have managed on my own."

"You don't buy it," he said.

"I don't know. I didn't have as much to lose then," I replied. "So I don't think I would have lost it so spectacularly."

"Maybe that proves my point more," he said. "That you feel pretty low, but you still sought out help. You have not lost what you've gained. You've got a self-awareness that struggles, but it's there, Annie. Give me another one."

"I lost Brody," the words slipped out. I'd been thinking about my mom, so it surprised even me.

"No," he said.

"What do you mean no?"

"I disagree," he replied.

"No shit. You can't disagree. You don't have the context of the conversation."

"You may need to apologize. You should even if you don't need to, but you haven't lost him," he said. "It's not that easy to push someone away. It may take effort. You'll have to fight her, but it's not over. Next. Come on. Give me the one I know you're holding back."

I sighed. He was right. "My mom's sick because of me."

"That's the most unreasonable," he said. "So it's going to be the hardest for you to bend on. How'd you get her sick? Was your cancer contagious?"

"She'd be healthier if I hadn't put her through so much," I mumbled. It was my subconscious, the voice inside my head that hated me so much, but it was more than that. I believed it too.

"You don't get cancer because you may get more colds than the average person," he said. "There's no correlation there, Annie."

"That doesn't matter."

"Of course it does," he shook his head. "Your mom thrives when she takes care of you. You are what she's most proud of. You always have been. You didn't get her sick. Her genes may have been partially responsible for you getting sick, however."

"Don't say that," I snapped.

"Genetically speaking, Annie... that is more likely. Absorb it. Let me know if you, not the bitch in your head— you—are willing to believe that in order to buy that you got her sick. Because statistically, I'm right."

"I will not blame her for getting sick, Matt," I bit my lip. "Fuck."

He was right. I struggled to process both statements as true. Logic was a way to bring me back in. It didn't mean that I hadn't become illogical. Anxiety was at its core illogical, but it helped ground me in what I believed instead of what the anxiety made me want to believe.

"Sometimes I hate when you're right," I grumbled.

"No, you don't," he said. "Annie. Seriously, I know you don't feel it, but your progress is astounding."

"Got any idea how to manage my dreams?" I said and it was as much of an acknowledgement as he was going to get that I agreed with him.

I didn't feel renewed. I was exhausted and sore, but the shame and guilt were manageable again. "Let's talk about it," he said. "Walk me through them."

● ● ●

Matt stayed with me through the afternoon, walking
me through mind-clearing exercises that would likely
help me shape my own dreams. I was desperate for
relief, exhausted but afraid to fall asleep and lose the
ground I'd regained, but by the time he left, I felt at
least a little assured I could manage it.

I took a long bath, picking up an old book that
had always sucked me in, and I read until the water
got cold. It was dinnertime, but I wasn't sure my
stomach would be able to handle food, and I was
contemplating trying something bland when there was
a knock at my door.

I didn't bother to act like I didn't wish it was
Brody. I really wanted it to be him, but when I found
Yvette on the other side, I wasn't disappointed. I'd
forgotten about her promise to stop by after work. She
had wine and takeout in hand and my stomach didn't
heave at the smell of Chinese, something I found
promising.

As happy as I was to see her, I wasn't ready to
talk again. I didn't feel like I had anything left to give.
"I've had a hell of a day," I told her. "I might need to
postpone."

"You don't have to tell me anything you don't
want to, Annie," she said easily. I could hear that
voice I pushed down, the one telling me that I didn't
deserve a friend like her, but Matt's time with me had
given me a good stranglehold on it for the time being.
"But you're at least helping me eat and drink
everything I brought."

"It's not that I don't want to," I said, plucking the
wine from her hands and allowing her to pass.

"I think I know that," she said softly. She
unbagged the cartons of food on my breakfast bar,
turning to me. "It's okay. I'm not going to be pushy
about any of this. I just want to hang out with my best

friend and watch *Scandal* in my pajamas. Sound good?"

I held her gaze for a moment. Her unyielding support was going to help me beat that voice in my head. "Sounds perfect."

DAY ELEVEN

Yvette and I stayed up half the night binge-watching *Scandal*, scarfing down fortune cookies and egg rolls on my bed, and getting drunk on wine. She asked nothing of me, not even anything about Brody. It had to have been killing her and I knew it, but I remained silent regardless. I wasn't ready and she was okay with it, and it helped to make me okay.

She worked late Sunday, but I had it off before an early Labor Day shift. We were both slow to wake up, slightly hungover from the wine, but my sleep had been blissfully silent. I hadn't dreamt about a thing, so headache or not, I felt renewed.

"Brunch?" Yvette asked through a yawn.

It was a smart idea. I needed to get out of my apartment and out of my own head for a little while. "Yeah."

"I'm using your shower."

"I'm making coffee," I replied.

"Praise Jesus," she grinned, rolling out of my bed and slipping into my tiny bathroom with her bag.

I brewed each of us a cup in my Keurig, opening my kitchen window wide. It was a beautiful late morning, sun streaming in, breeze warm and inviting. I picked out my outfit based entirely on the weather, landing on an army green summer dress, denim vest, and sneakers. In front of the mirror by my front door, I wove my hair into a braid and pulled it over my shoulder.

Yvette nodded her approval when she popped out of the bathroom, wearing a sleeveless chambray shirt and olive green pants. We looked like we'd coordinated and it made me burst out laughing. I moved to my closet to change again, but she stopped me. "Don't fight it, Annie. We're meant to be."

I snorted, but shrugged. I was comfortable, Yvette looked as gorgeous as she always did, and I was ready for bacon and eggs.

Yvette drove us to the Buttered Tin in Saint Paul. It was her favorite brunch spot and I never cared, bacon and eggs being bacon and eggs no matter where I got it. She was behind her menu, contemplating her options, when I opened my mouth to speak.

The words that tumbled out weren't the ones I'd expected. "I ran Brody off," I told her.

She dropped the menu to the table, sighing softly. The server took that moment to appear, asking for our drink order, and Yvette ordered screwdrivers for both of us.

"Oh Annie," she shook her head. "Why?"

"You should hear it in here," I joked, tapping on my temple. "I didn't have a choice. Or it didn't feel like it at the time."

She eyed me for a moment. "You sound like you regret it."

"I do," I admitted.

"Then why are you here with me right now, not begging for his forgiveness?"

"I'm afraid I'll do it again," I said. "My control is not great."

"What happened, Annie?" she asked me. "Because that's not what had you so off-balance before. You were off before he even showed up. You're leaving something out that probably matters, right?"

"My mom's sick," I blurted out. "She told me yesterday."

Yvette opened and closed her mouth several times, not coming up with the words she wanted to say, and I didn't blame her. "You mean cancer, right?" I closed my eyes and nodded. "Are you *fucking* kidding me? Like you and Mama Jenkins haven't been through enough?"

"That basically summarizes how I feel about it," I admitted, giving her a small smile. As horrible as it was, there was something important in her validation of my feelings. I was right to be upset, even slightly unhinged.

"You found that out and got him back on the same day?" Yvette asked after our drinks were dropped and we ordered our food.

"It's fucking unfair, Evie," I said. The words burst out of their own accord, but that didn't make them any less true. "I just—I can't handle—I'm doomed to fail at this."

"Because you don't think you deserve anything good," she said pointedly. "I can make this make sense, Annie. You just found out your mom's sick with what defined your entire life, and your prince charming shows up, the same one that knew you from before… you think *he* doesn't get it?" she shook her head. "He gets it."

"I'm broken," I said. "I'm better than I ever was. I am. I can admit that. But I am not whole. I'll never be whole."

"Who is?" Yvette asked. "I don't have your life. I don't have your examples of when life really screws you over, but that doesn't mean I haven't felt my own version of it too. My best friend disappeared from my life for seven years. On its own, that was enough, but I was the only non-white person in the entire school district, Annie. We're all broken. We all break, and put ourselves back together, and find a way to move on, to carry on until maybe we get broken again, but come on—it's living. It's life. We get one shot at it. Not everything's going to be perfect, but at this point, you have to have experienced all of the horrible shit you're due for."

There were tears behind my eyes, the kind that could easily push over. "Everything should be golden now?"

"For you, everything should be perfect, Annie," she squeezed my hands. "You, at this point, can demand perfection. From yourself. From the people you surround yourself with."

I closed my eyes for a moment. "I saw him without his shirt on," I finally spoke. "I had perfection right in front of me."

She burst out laughing, nearly spewing her drink all over me. "Then why are you here?"

"Because you are more important than he is. This is more important. He can wait."

• • •

We lazed our way through brunch, staying way too long, but I wanted her company and I knew she was nervous about letting me go without her. I felt okay thanks to Matt and Yvette. I could think about my mom without the rising panic and that was mostly because they helped me to understand that feeling upset and panicked was completely normal. Completely normal, but not in any way my fault.

The voice in my head wasn't silent. She was never going to be silent, but I had a hold on her. I wasn't going to hide from the friendship Yvette could give me. She was never going to let me anyway.

She was quiet on the ride back to my apartment. I knew she was worried about me, so I let her work through her thoughts, my mind drifting.

"Don't hate me," she said, giving me a small smile as she pulled off onto Midway Parkway from Snelling, directly across from the State Fair entrance. "But you need to talk to him. And not because you need a boy to make you happy, Annie. Because you

154

deserve the opportunity to explore what you should have had all along."

I squeezed my eyes shut. "Okay," I said slowly. She knew how to say things the way I needed to hear them. I'd become remarkably self-sufficient—maybe even to a fault—but I didn't want to give it up. I was proud of what I was capable of on my own and she knew how I wouldn't just give that away. After reconnecting with Brody, however brief, however much I'd overreacted, I wanted one more shot. I wanted to explain myself. I wanted him to know me as much as I wanted to know him, and I hadn't felt that way about anyone since I'd met him the first time.

"If you need me," she said. "You call me. You understand me on that?"

I nodded. "I'm okay. I'll be okay."

"But if you're not," she said. "If it doesn't play out the way you expect and you need a friend, you know where to find me. And I demand that you do it."

"I will," I assured her. "You're stuck with me now. I won't run away unless you do."

She reached for my hand and squeezed it tightly. "We've both had that happen to us, honey. I'm not doing it to you, so you've pretty much got me for the long haul." She squeezed me again. "Now get out of my car and go."

I snorted and complied. "Let me know how it goes," she shouted after me. "And take your hair out of that braid!" I waved a hand in acknowledgment and I headed towards the entrance of the fair, sighing softly to myself as I undid my hair.

I didn't have my MINMIC credentials, but I wouldn't have used them if I did. I paid the admission and followed the Saturday crowd inside.

It was beautiful, the perfect late summer day that was warm but breezy enough not to be hot. There were people everywhere, impossible to avoid, but after ten straight days on the grounds, I knew the best ways to avoid the crowds, and besides a few shortcuts, I took the most direct path to the Flowering Onion stand as I could.

I had no idea if he was there. I had my phone and could have called, but after everything, finding him where I'd been looking for so long seemed right.

"He's not here," Chelsey, Brody's blonde friend, said from the other side of the booth. She was sweaty and busy, but her voice was kind. I was caught off guard, though I wasn't completely sure if her tone or his absence was why. "His shift starts at three," she added. "If you want to hang around."

"Thank you," I replied, slipping away from the booth so she could work. It was just over an hour until three, but I had no desire to explore the fair any further. I could have gone to the MINMIC booth, but it took a different kind of courage to talk to strangers about mental illness than it did to talk to someone that mattered to me about mine. I watched a family leave a bench next to the stand, so I took a spot at the end of it, knowing the only way to keep my head in the game was to stay nearby.

I paid attention to the people who sat beside me on the bench, couples and families and other singletons like me, all taking a break from the hubbub around them. Their emotions ran the gambit—from irritated to breathtaken to hopelessly in love. It reminded me in some ways of what the hospital had been like, the comings and goings of people I never got to know that well, of so many strong emotions wrapped up into each person. It was fascinating to watch it again and the familiarity of it grounded me.

At quarter to three, I got a whiff of onions and a flash of yellow in my periphery. Chelsey sat down beside me, gulping down a bottle of water. "You hurt him," she said, but there was no bite to her tone.

"I know," I said. "That's what I'm here to rectify. If I can."

She looked at me for a moment. She really was beautiful, even after spending a week in a grease trap. Her blonde hair was in a messy bun, a red visor keeping the hair out of her face. Her eyes were a bright aquamarine; she was slim, but strong. And he didn't want her.

"I've known Wash for years," she said. "I moved to Lakeville my junior year of high school. He was a senior. Him and Kevin. And it's been the three of us since then. I didn't learn about Gwen until he left for college. I learned about you at the same time." She shook her head. "I had a game. I was okay with the long one. Eventually he might have figured it out, but when he ran into you here last week? It was over. It's over. It's only ever been you."

My heart thumped in my chest and I squeezed my hands tightly together. "I'm sorry?" I said, but it came out like a question, and we both laughed.

"For the record, I'm not usually this chill," she said. "But I love him. Maybe in too many ways, but the way I mean doesn't hurt. I just want him happy. I've seen the dark side of him—it's what drew me to him to start with—but he's not meant to be dark. He shines. It's stupid. I feel like an idiot, but he shines more with you. So just... let him." she said.

She noticed him before I did, rising to her feet, and I felt abruptly terrified. He approached us both, but he gave us a suspiciously wide berth, and though I could make out that I'd hurt him, his mask was a strong one. "I'm taking your shift," Chelsey told him. Her tone left no room for argument, and though his eyes widened, he didn't try. "Not usually this chill," she reminded me. She squeezed his shoulder briefly before she disappeared back inside the booth.

I opened and closed my mouth several times, looking at him in yellow again. My mouth was dry, my cheeks were warm, and I was such an idiot. "I am so sorry," I said vehemently.

His expression didn't change; he was as unreadable as he'd ever been to me. "Can we get out of here?" he asked, glancing over my shoulder at where I assumed Chelsey was standing.

I nodded, but said nothing else. I let him lead the way, following directly behind him through the melee of bodies. We were past the gates, the same ones I'd come through, before there was enough space for the two of us to stand side by side.

He said nothing as he walked. He seemed to have a destination so I followed him, heart racing. The silence was heavy, though not awkward, and I knew that he was processing, trying to determine what he wanted to say, and I had no desire to rush him. I also wanted to be facing each other when it was time for me to admit everything I'd been through in a less accusatory way. None of it made me less nervous, though. I was still terrified that he'd decide there was no point in dealing with my drama.

We stopped abruptly in front of a house on Iowa Street. It was a cute one-story, white with black shutters and sunflowers and a neatly manicured lawn and I bit down hard on my lip when I realized he'd brought me home.

I followed him up the walk towards his red door. I said nothing as he unlocked it and opened the door to allow me inside. It was full of light, tidy but not completely clean. He grabbed a few articles of clothing off his couch, deposited a couple of dishes into his dishwasher, before he finally spoke. "I'm going to change," he said. He disappeared down a hallway and I heard a door shut before I let out the shaky breath I'd been holding since I saw him.

I distracted myself with the photos in his living room. There were a few of his parents, one of him and Chelsey and Kevin at what looked to be a wedding, but my eyes skimmed right past that as I landed on one of Gwen. I didn't have anything besides my memory—I hadn't for either of them—but just like I hadn't forgotten what Brody had looked like, I never would forget Gwen either. In the picture, she had a purple scarf wrapped around her head, one I'd gotten for her. I had a matching one in green. She was smiling widely, looking as radiant as ever, and I remembered what she was laughing at because it had been me. Brody had taken a lot of pictures that day. It was only a week before she died, but the three of us had been happy.

I pushed on the corner of my eye, picking up the photo to take even more of it in. Brody ducked out of his bedroom, in dark denim and a deep red shirt, and I realized it was the first time I'd seen him in anything other than yellow in ten years.

"Brody," I said softly. I had no idea what the next words out of my mouth were going to be, but I didn't need them. His body language was different, open and wary and excited and devastated all rolled into one so I did the thing I would have wanted myself and I hugged him.

He shuddered against me, his arms tight around me, and I let him fold me against him on his leather couch. I sat between his legs, my back pressed against his right leg and the arm of the couch. My knees arched over his left leg, and my side rested against his chest, my head resting perfectly in the crook of his neck.

"How do we still fit together like this?" he asked, his lips against my hair.

I chuckled. We had fit together well even when I was sick. I was small, all bones, but he was growing, bulking out, and he could embrace me nearly completely. I'd felt like a cocooned caterpillar with him when I was a preteen, in a bubble of safety that I didn't think I'd be able to get back once he was gone, and I realized I'd nearly abolished that feeling on purpose.

"I'm so sorry," I said again.

"Don't be sorry," he said. "I think I can piece together a lot of what you tried to say earlier, but I'd rather you just started from the beginning." I nodded, but I had no idea where to begin. Matt had helped me with a lot, but I'd spoken to Brody with the intent of causing him pain. Undoing that didn't seem easy.

"Annie," he said quietly. I raised my head to meet his gaze and he captured my mouth with his. My hands couldn't stay still, slipping up to his neck, and he pulled back shakily. "I could get very easily distracted here," he grinned. "But that wasn't the point. The point is that there's nothing that you have to prove. There's nothing you have to do. I'm already in. I'm not letting you go again. I was going to show up on your doorstep tonight if you hadn't shown up on mine."

"Why?" I said, the word slipping out on its own. It's what I wanted to know, probably more than anything, but I hadn't intended to ask it.

"Because I let you go ten years ago and have spent a decade wondering 'what if'. A decade, Annie. And ten seconds into finding you again and I knew I'd been the world's biggest idiot," he shook his head, wrapping my hair around his fingers. "Ten years and I haven't wanted anyone but you. So I'm not stupid enough to spit in the face of that twice."

I pushed my hand to his heart. "I could have died. I came close to dying. Twice." His body tensed. "Would you have what-ifed this forever?"

"I wish I could say no, but... I don't know," he said. "It would have been in the back of my mind forever, I think." He nudged my forehead with his chin. "Tell me," he said softly.

I did. I told him everything I had dumped on him before, but in chronological order and without so much pain. It still hurt, the fear and the loneliness and the guilt, but I wasn't spewing it out of shame, so he was able to gain insight into all of the things I'd been through without having to feel any sense of responsibility for them.

"Annie," he said when I finished talking about my mother. His grip on me was tight, his voice heavy with the same sadness and fear that I felt, and it was my turn to kiss him.

After putting myself through the wringer, I was less reserved than he had been. I shifted so that I was fully facing him, straddling his lap, dress riding up. I shrugged out of my denim vest and his fingers against the nape of my neck were intoxicating. His lips were as insistent as mine, but he was the one to break it off, breathing heavily against my collarbone.

"Thinking about kissing you made me survive chemo," I admitted and he laughed. "It's true," I insisted. "I needed something good in my head, and I always came back to being with you." It was true, even well beyond the point where I felt mostly anger at him for abandoning me. When I needed something good in the moment, he was my fallback. Remembering how I'd felt when he'd touch me was worth thinking of, even if everything about it hurt.

"I used to do that too," he smiled. "Though I was crueler to myself as I got older—I'd think about all of the even innocent places I'd been too nervous to touch."

"Oh?" I said, heart pounding. "Like where?"

He traced my collarbone with his fingertips and my eyes closed instinctually. His mouth followed the same path as his fingers, his lips pressing feather light kisses to my collarbone, and after a moment, his large hands came to rest tentatively high on my thighs. He pushed his forehead to mine for a moment before he wrapped me in a hug again. "I want to tell you about me," he said, his voice not completely even. "But can I ask one more question?"

"You can ask whatever you want," I said, my fingers finding a bare swath of skin above the hem of his jeans.

"You're distracting me," he admitted and I chuckled, clasping my hands together. "What happened that morning?" he asked and I knew what he meant. He wanted to know if he'd set me off.

"I have nightmares," I explained. It was an easy answer to start with, but it would become invariably harder as I kept talking. "In the timeline of everything I've been through, they're relatively new. My emotions get jumbled and I can't straighten it out, and I woke up with you and all I could think was that I didn't deserve anything good." His grip tightened on me. "I haven't lost it like that in a long time. I called my old therapist and we walked through it, but that part is going to be a journey, Brody. I'm trying. But I have to constantly try and sometimes that's exhausting. All the time that's exhausting. I'm not always good at staying in control." I didn't want to look at him, not as the silence grew longer, but I was glad that I'd told him the truth. I didn't want him to think it wouldn't happen again. It probably would.

He kissed my hair again. "I want to come back to that, but it'll be easier after I tell you what the last ten years were like for me. We're not all that different, Annie. Or," he amended. "You went through a lot more, but I got just as—"

"Dark," I supplied. He nodded in surprise. "That's what Chelsey said. I'm not running away. But I am epically bad at saying the wrong thing. I had a lot of time alone."

He tensed and I realized he was blaming himself for that. "Like that," I pointed out and he relaxed. "I'm sad we lost all this time, but I got past angry a long time ago. There's no way to separate it from the anger I had about being sick, or all those hormones, or the beginning of my slide into depression. Control what I can control and all that—I'm not holding myself to unrealistic expectations anymore." I shook my head. "And meet my therapist. I just word vomited out his best phrases. He'd be proud," I smiled at him. "Anyway, we are supposed to be talking about you."

He was quiet again, but his body language was still inviting and he was still holding me against him like he had no plans to let me go, so I let him process his thoughts while I tried to slow my racing heart. I didn't know how it felt exactly like it had when we were kids, but the thrill and the hope were so clear that I couldn't deny it.

"When Gwen died," he said. "I shut down. I turned off. I—thinking about it now, when it hurts less, after processing so much of it, I still struggle to remember exactly what I did during the first couple of months after her death. I scared the shit out of my parents—I know that. They'd lost Gwen, and they couldn't reach me at all. And now, it really feels like I went somewhere. Somewhere I don't remember. I think I just wanted to be where she was. So I disconnected. From them. From you. It took months before I snapped out of it.

"It was near her birthday," he continued. I felt as far into the past as he did. Our stories didn't come together again, but they were parallel in a lot of ways. What he was saying was familiar. "My mom mentioned you."

"What?" I blurted out. I hadn't been expecting that at all.

"She wasn't even talking to me," he admitted. "She and my step-dad were talking, they were trying to find out how to fix me. She thought about you, but after Gwen, she…"

"She didn't know what to do with me," I said, shaking my head. "Not after she inevitably thought it. *I* thought it."

"Thought what?"

"That she wished it would have been me," I said, shrugging. "She didn't know how to deal with me or my mom after that. And I'm not mad about it for me, but for my mom, I am—a little. For what it's worth."

"I don't blame you," he said softly.

"It was all about survival. It's okay," I said. "But how did that help?"

"I never thought it," he said. "Not once. But losing you voluntarily, at the time, was a hell of a lot better than having to send you into an OR and never see you again. I couldn't—that wasn't something I could fathom, so I ran. It was intentional. It was self-serving. And lo and behold, once I realized my parents were considering bringing you around again, I came out of it enough so that it didn't happen."

He drifted into silence again. My feelings weren't hurt, but there was some residual pain left over after that kind of abandonment. "It was the worst choice I've ever made, Annie," he said. "And I'm sure that sounds cheesy and unbelievable, but… even in spite of this—" he gestured between us, "—in spite of us ever connecting again, it was. I thought about you constantly, and I started to hate myself for everything I'd done, or hadn't done."

"You got dark," I said after a moment.

He nodded. "Two weeks after the first anniversary of her death, I got in a fight at school. I remember every stupid second of it. I beat the shit out of some kid for cutting in the cafeteria line. It wasn't even worth anything. And I remember how I felt when I did it, this sense of power and release..." he shook his head. "It terrified me more than anything, but it also intrigued me enough..." he trailed off. "I knew there was something wrong. I was sixteen with a dead sister, but I was also a hell of an athlete, so I got lucky. They directed me towards sports—my principal pushed me at football as a way to manage my anger. In retrospect, it was dangerous as hell to give my anger that kind of stage, but I was still scared of it." He glanced down at me. "I'm past this though, Annie. I'm jumping ahead because I don't know if I could handle you being afraid of me."

"I'm not afraid of you," I told him immediately. It was true, and it wasn't a product of any of my bad judgment. I knew rage well, and mine felt much closer to the surface than his did. He had been through things I could relate to and he had progressed far enough on his own path that he could talk about it. I was not afraid of him.

"I started as a defensive player," he said. "I was too tall, not bulky enough to be a linesman, so they put me on the corners, and I would annihilate receivers. I loved it. I was good at it. But the penalties weren't good for the team, and there was a..." he sucked in a breath. "I hit someone hard during a practice game—harder than I ever needed to, but that was the only way I hit then—and knocked him out cold. It took just long enough to wake him up that the coaching staff was beginning to get worried. They laid him perfectly flat—I won't forget this—because they thought I might have broken his neck."

I squeezed his hands between mine. His horror was fresh; it had been probably seven or eight years, but his reaction was one of genuine pain. "The first thing that moron said when he came to was to ask if that was all I had," he shook his head, but his tone was light. "Kev and I switched positions. I moved to receiver, then tight end, and he got to smash me up in return for a while. And I was better as a tight end. Suddenly I was being scouted, so I played smarter, not harder, and it got me a free ride to NDSU... and Kev and Chels, they helped me manage. I tried therapy, but it just made me edgy. I tried yoga on a whim—trying to impress a girl I still wanted to be you." I snorted. "Couldn't turn her into you, but it was exactly what I needed otherwise." He looked at me. "You think I'm kidding."

"I think it's been ten years," I said. "And you could have found me if you wanted to."

He shook his head. "I had this idea built up in my head. About you, about... what we could be. Finding you on Facebook—it didn't mesh with any of it. Ten years, Annie. You weren't still thinking about me. I wasn't ready for the devastation."

"And you are now?" I raised my eyebrows.

"First," he cupped my cheek with his hand, "This isn't devastation. This is incredible." He bent his head down to kiss me and I gripped his tee shirt tightly. "Second, the universe kept pushing us together. I wasn't going to deny it the chance."

"Except with Juan," I pointed out.

"I panicked," he said. "I kissed you that night completely without thought, and I let Kev and Chelsey lead me away because I didn't know what else to do. I'd run through this situation hundreds of times—casually running into you—but I hadn't accounted for that initial awkwardness and it made me think I was all wrong. I kissed you because I had to do it again, one more time, and then I saw you with him and I… I thought that was it. I thought we'd had our shot and I'd fucked it up out of fear and the world wanted me to know that. I don't know. I've never been rational when it comes to how I feel about you."

"And then I freaked out and kicked you out," I pointed out. "Maybe we're reading these signs wrong."

"I ran into you again. Complete fluke, again. And you were so much like the you I remembered that I knew I'd wait around forever," he said. "And then you let me hold you, and touch you, and kiss you, and sleep next to you, and you thought you have the ability to run me off again? Not gonna happen."

I released his shirt to push on the corners of my eyes. The dark parts of my mind were still silent—there was no voice telling me what I didn't deserve, what I wasn't worth—and that silence was the most reassuring thing I'd felt in years. "This was always going to be how our story ended," he said. "The two of us, better and stronger together. Whether Gwen died or not. Whether you were ever even sick. Our paths were going to wind together. Do you feel that?"

I shook my head, capturing his lips with mine. His hands wound into my hair, mine slipped under his shirt, and I was gasping when we broke apart. "It's not how our story ends, Brody. It's how it starts."

Day Twelve…

About the Author

Kayli Schaaf lives in Minnesota. She never misses the Great Minnesota Get-Together.

Made in the USA
Lexington, KY
29 August 2018